PAPER
HANGAR

A NOVEL WRITTEN BY

SHANE KAMMERDIENER

Paper Hangar

Published by Thomas S. Kammerdiener

ISBN: 978-0-9989218-0-8

All characters in this book are fiction and figments of the author's imagination.

Paper Hanger-- Slang --A con man who passes bad cheques or counterfeit paper money; a forger, a con artist.

CHAPTER 1

September 3, 2008 10:00 a.m.

Finally, a relaxing drive. The pressure, sleepless nights, and anger should finally dissipate. As I walk into Pete's Bar in Neptune Beach, I'm welcomed by an old familiar stench of stale beer and smoke.

The last few years of chronic stress brought on by massive loads of unending paperwork have finally taken their toll. My former boss is likely still trying to figure out what happened.

Reflecting on the chaos caused by my dramatic office departure, I feel a deep sense of satisfaction descend upon me.

The first taste of a fresh Heineken draft is almost more than I can take. The jukebox is blaring an old Bon Jovi song, and I realize I haven't had this feeling in a decade, adding to an almost overwhelming sense of relief. Years of sobriety had left me overly concerned with things that don't matter and worried about things that never happened. All I can do now is laugh. My tie is somewhere on A1A, and my Armani suit jacket's in a dumpster next to the Lemon Bar.

The absurd reality hit me sometime last week. Looking in the mirror had become my morning nightmare. The drive to the office was grueling. The combined smell of cheap cologne, perfume and cigarettes told me of another day in office hell. This wasn't the life I'd planned to live when I left college. Flying, adventure, certainly not boredom, were what I'd set my sights on. Even the lustful smile of Nikki, my boss's wife, didn't relieve the nauseous thought of another day of work—and my fear of one day going postal was ever-present. It was time to get out.

Last night's departure from the office lit the fuse to my explosive exit. My boss, John Marris, had just dropped another five files on my desk with the expectation that the underwriting work, appraisals and final sign-offs be completed in a week. His last words to me that night were, "I'll expect to see you at the office early tomorrow morning, Pete." Normally he's a late arrival. While that would usually add stress to my already stress-packed corporate life, it didn't. In an instant, I decided I was never going to comply. Fuck his expectations. I packed up my briefcase, went through the office file cabinet and pulled out two boxes of the highest dollar deals my office was processing, and went home. "Good luck hitting your quota this month, prick!" I said to myself.

This morning I walked into the office listening to a shiny, new iPod. My dancing must have looked a little crazy to those who couldn't hear the music. It should have been a clue that something was amiss. Life as usual, in an office hotbox full of cubicles, no one even noticed. Everyone continued doing what they do, utterly oblivious to my temporary insanity.

Nikki noticed but continued with her mundane morning duties. When I motioned for her to meet me in the conference room, she gave me a coy gaze and obliged. She wasn't expecting her husband for another hour, but I knew better—his plan was to meet me for an early morning work session.

Surprised delight appeared on her face when I brushed my hand across her buttocks and pulled her close to me. "Oh Pete," she cooed. It only took a second for her to reciprocate. After only a few more seconds John Marris, her husband, my boss, walked in. For dramatic effect I slid my hand down the back of her tiny little ass and gripped it firmly as a look of crimson, stupefied shock crawled up his face. "Not what you were expecting eh, asshole?"

"Another day in paradise," I said to her as I popped open a can of Mountain Dew and walked out smiling nonchalantly. John screaming, "You fuckin' bitch," was heard all the way down the hall. The sound of my laughter could be heard just as far.

As I left the office, I couldn't help but smile, thinking about Nikki. She's gorgeous—but married. Unhappily—but married nevertheless. We've had this on again-off again, taboo fling going on almost a year. For me, it's just been about thinking of my asshole boss, silently laughing in his face knowing I'm screwing his wife. I'm not sure what it was for her. I've often wondered what her motivation was. In the end, I just didn't care. And at this point, it really doesn't matter.

Twenty minutes after leaving the office, I've got an ice cold beer in front of me. It's 10 a.m. My life in corporate America is now over and I begin to think about a future with no corporate politics, pricks, meetings, or conference calls. Going out in style has never felt better.

So today I drink at Pete's. I walk the beach, listen to the waves crashing on the sand, and try to formulate a plan taking me no further than tomorrow.

CHAPTER 2

September 4, 2008 11:00 a.m.

The truck's loaded. Cowboy hat, cooler, and cassette tapes are all within easy reach. While enduring the stinging hangover instilled by yesterday's release from sobriety, an awesome song comes on the radio. Kenny Chesney's "Spirit of a Storm" begins blaring through the half-blown speakers of my 1997 Ford pickup. If ever there was a song that fits how I feel, this is it.

Pulling out of my condo with the radio crankin', I finally feel the weight of life lifting. Since laying waste to the marital bliss of the luscious Nikki yesterday, I have no responsibilities—zero— and I feel great. But that's not the way I've been feeling for the last couple of years. It's time to unwind, disengage, and let it all go.

Many years ago, I enjoyed traveling to new places, often at the controls of an airplane. I still do. But this time I feel the need to visit familiar places and retrace steps from the past, trying to recall who I once was. After months of unrelenting work pressure, financial stress, and human drama, I long for quiet days in familiar surroundings.

So I head south. My destination: Key West. There's no better place to fall off the face of the earth. But first things first. Cocoa

Beach is just a few miles down A1A, and I know the place well. I lived there for a short time after graduating from college. I check into the Hilton and take a stroll down the beach to a local oyster bar in search of an aphrodisiac and a little companionship. Luckily, I find them both, and after a steamy morning romp with a willing and sexy black chick, I pop in a stick of Bazooka Joe and resume the drive to my falling-off spot.

The Seven-Mile Bridge is a special place for me. I first laid eyes on it in the summer of 1986. It links Marathon Key to the lower keys and the Conch Republic. I both flew and drove over it many times years ago. It marks your arrival to a place of release, peace, music, and, hopefully for me, amnesia. I know when I cross that landmark, time stands still. For in Key West, nothing really matters except good friends, good songs, and good liquor—all of which are in plentiful supply.

I pull off onto Knights Key Boulevard before crossing the bridge. The Sunset Grille and Bar seems the perfect place for a mood adjustment before easing my way into the lower keys. I belly up to the bar and order a pitcher of the local brew. Time flies and the sun sets as I get back in the truck and head over the bridge. I crank up a country music station and suddenly find myself laughing hysterically about the last few days. As I drive, I look over and notice the two boxes of work files. I roll down both windows, reach over and grab a stack and throw them out the window. It energizes me, so I toss more. Before long I'm wildly throwing them as fast as I can. I can't imagine what it looks like to the cars traveling behind me, but I couldn't care less. It feels great. By the time I regain composure, both boxes are empty.

It doesn't take long and I've arrived at Key West. Fortunately, the South Breeze Motel's perpetual revolving door never ceases to turn, and it seems a clean room forever awaits my arrival. Even though I haven't been here in years, it seems they can predict my next visit. Telepathy maybe.

A short walk across the street and I rent my bike for the week, and head off to the Hog's Breath for Round 1. It's karaoke night and the place is packed with just what I need: a swarm of good-looking revelers—the exact opposite of what Pete's had to offer two days ago.

As a young man, I always found that perspective seemed to change when I was at sea level viewing life through the bottom of an empty glass. Add some unique, melodic island music, and life's a little sunnier already. I hope time away will soothe that uncomfortable feeling of not knowing what to do, when to do it, or how to fix the mistakes I've made. I need to slow down, decompress, and melt into an old worn-out beach chair. This tiny American island has always been the perfect medicine for me. With a little luck, it will be again.

CHAPTER 3

September 6, 2008 10:00 a.m.

For some reason, I feel the need to turn on my Blackberry this morning and listen to what was sure to be a mountain of messages. I'd shut it off three days ago when I left the office. With no intention of returning a call, I crack open a beer, spike it with whiskey and turn up the volume for maximum enjoyment. The first three are from Nikki. I never knew I had so many descriptive nicknames. I laugh so hard my stomach hurts. The others are various colleagues. All had real estate deals in midstream and were scrambling to cover their asses. They assume correctly that they have big problems. Their files were strewn across U.S. 1 somewhere near Boca Chica Channel.

Luckily, my bike is parked in front of my room. I have no recollection of leaving it there. As I head out to eat, the hotel manager chastises me for my late night singing. I guess he doesn't care for Hank Williams Jr. Funny, they didn't seem to mind it at the Hog's Breath. I pedal my way down Duval Street, unsure of whether I'm drunk or hungover. One thing's for certain—I feel no stress. Dante's Raw Bar is one of my favorite places, and it's just down the street. It has a pool, sexy waitresses, and good food.

I take a stool and order a beer. Cuban girls have always intrigued me. Since the bartender, Adriana, speaks like she just got off the boat, I may have hit the jackpot. I sit, I drink, and I drool.

Recalling a message from the blackberry, I begin to wonder if trouble could find me here in Key West. My ex boss left a voicemail telling me to watch my back. I don't blame him. After all, his marriage is over, my pilfering of the company files cost him at least $100,000 in bonus money, and I laughed in his face when he caught me with his wife. With his job most likely gone, he has nothing to do except look for me. While a civil suit against me might carry weight, it's doubtful he'd be able to garner enough assistance from law enforcement to track me down. I dismiss the thought and continue enjoying a tray of raw oysters and gulping lager from a frosty mug.

With daylight fading and a full day of poolside debauchery drawing to a close, Adriana kindly cuts off my alcohol I.V. I stumble off the stool and ride toward a place called Mallory Square. It's a quaint little historic area on the west end of the island where a carnival type festival occurs every evening in celebration of the sunset. The festival is in full swing so I sit and watch the tourists, the performers, and the airplanes flying overhead toward Key West International. My mind wanders back to the days when I had no worries. When all I cared about was flying, making money, and partying. This empty feeling I've been experiencing didn't exist in those days. Something caused it, but the cause eludes me.

The sun has burned out and I decide to call it a day. Four days of drinking have begun to take a toll. Instead of waking up on a park bench, I meander toward the South Breeze, stopping along the way for another drink or two. My iPod is at full volume when I turn the corner bringing the motel office into view. Two men are close to the manager, and it doesn't appear to be a friendly exchange. I begin singing loudly, and ride my bike directly into the middle of them all. Acting more inebriated than I really am, I fall into the two men I don't recognize and pretend to be a sorry drunk. They back off just enough for me to get up and fall into them again. Suddenly, I pull the smaller of the two to the ground and hold him there. The motel manager, an old guy named Gavin I met when I checked in a couple of days ago, moves toward the other man and smashes him against the office door. Suddenly, a Key West Police cruiser rounds the corner and two uniformed officers jump in. They cuff the man Gavin has incapacitated. When they jump on top of me and the other guy, Gavin rushes to my aid, telling the officers I'm helping him. I roll over, laughing in a state of drunkenness, and formally introduce myself. Gavin laughs too and says thanks. He says these guys are street bums who occasionally try to cheat mom and pop motels out of a free room. A friend at another motel had alerted him. When he saw them, he immediately called the cops. I just happened to roll up before they arrived.

After the mêlée, Gavin locks up the office and hands me a beer. He says I earned it. I tell him thanks and we strike up a conversation. It's mostly small talk, but by the end I'm slurring my words, obviously done for the day. Gavin's a jovial old guy with a wonderful demeanor. It's nice to make a friend.

CHAPTER 4

September 7, 2008 8:00 a.m.

I'm awakened by the sound of Gavin pounding on my door requesting the help I'd volunteered last night during my drunken stupor. He needs assistance replacing an air conditioner. Although nursing a four-day hangover is not conducive to heavy lifting, with nothing else on my agenda, I oblige. He brings along his only employee and assures me we'll be done in a few hours. The guy's name is Rob, a scraggly looking Key West type in his mid- thirties. When I open the door, Rob laughs in my face and informs me I look like hell. Forcing a smile, I tell him to kiss my ass. He chuckles and leads me to his work truck.

Why did I volunteer for this? These problems never came up when I was sober. I would simply ignore a request or say no. Alcohol seems to make me friendlier.

I sweat profusely while we work and Rob just keeps questioning me about why I am here and how long I'll be staying. He says Gavin found me humorous and enjoyed having me at the motel. I wish he'd just shut up. But I listen and make conversation. Soon we're done. The work actually relieves my hangover.

It turns out to be enjoyable, even though Rob talked incessantly. Strangely, it feels nice to help.

I decide to pay Gavin for a couple of weeks at the motel. I need to unload some cash, and it seems Gavin could use it. When I approach him, he's happy to take my money and seems glad I'll be around for a while. He's careful not to ask too many questions, but I sense his curiosity. Rightfully so. I'm alone, paying for two weeks in cash and can't give him the vaguest idea of how long I plan on staying. He says thanks for my earlier assistance and wishes me a good day on the island.

It's getting late in the day so I head to Dante's for a visit with Adriana. In her thick Cuban accent, she laughs and calls me a "pussy" when I order water. I can't help being attracted to her strong personality. I chuckle, unable to recall a woman ever referring to me as a pussy. I order some oysters and watch the news on the overhead TV. Since it's a slow day at the bar, we have time to chat. The story of her arrival in America nearly brings me to tears. She'd boarded a small dinghy in Cuba and made the transit across the Florida Straits, coming ashore somewhere near Marathon Key. Two of the five people in her boat died during the crossing. She tells me she'd left to escape persecution from Castro, who had her father killed. Her mother had died from natural causes shortly thereafter. Since her brother had made the journey years ago, and her parents were now deceased, she decided to try it. That was a year ago and she ended up settling in Key West. Her brother resides in Miami. Adriana has a genuineness about her that appeals to me. I haven't seen it in anyone for a long time. She doesn't seem to want anything from me—and it doesn't matter to her where I'm from or what I'm doing here.

After a while, an inebriated tourist from New York sits down next to me. She's a tiny woman with perfectly sculpted breasts.

She's friendly in that drunken, horny sort of way and before I know it, we're off to her hotel. I wink at Adriana as I leave. She gives me an ornery little smile as she shakes her head.

After a couple of hours, her annoying Northeastern accent got old, perfect tits or no. I pull on my flowered swim trunks and tell her she talks too much. As the door closes, I can hear the muffled sound of her voice calling me an "asshole." "Another satisfied customer," I laugh to myself as I head for home.

I quietly roll up to the South Breeze and park my bike. No singing tonight, so Gavin has nothing to scold me about. He's sitting on a bench in front of the motel and thanks me again for helping out earlier this morning. I tell him I was glad to help and my only complaint was that Rob wouldn't shut up. I say it with a smile, careful not to offend him. He immediately looks me in the eye and tells me not to be fooled; Rob is smart and loyal. He says Rob has been here for a long time and is welcome to stay as long as he wishes. We talk for a bit and then call it a night.

CHAPTER 5

September 9, 2008 4:00 p.m.

The next two days pass with little fanfare. I stay away from alcohol, relax at the hotel pool and make a daily run to Dante's. I'm relaxing and beginning to think about what I might do in the future.

It's late afternoon when I head out to see Adriana and take a dip at the pool. I arrive to find Rob sitting at the bar so I pull up a stool next to him and order us both a beer. Adriana serves me water with my beer and shoots me a sly wink. I'm surprised to feel my heart skip a beat.

Rob seems perplexed but asks no questions. The TV is turned to Fox News Channel and since I hadn't watched it in a few days, I give it some attention. Rob and I talk about Key West and how he'd come to call it home. He moved here in the mid-'90s with his family. His parents moved to Tampa after he graduated from high school, but he stayed on the island. He'd taken a job with a company delivering boats to the Bahamas. The money was good—"Too good," he says. If not for getting busted with a full load of marijuana, he tells me he'd still be doing it. I listen but ask no questions. His story is interesting but I sense he's holding back. I don't press him. I feel comfortable telling him I'd just become unemployed up in Jacksonville and am in Key West to blow off some steam, relax, and recharge a bit. We have a couple more beers when Adriana serves up a shot.

The Fox News anchor suddenly catches my attention talking about my former employer, Thrift Bank Mortgage. I'm shocked when I see footage of my office in Jacksonville. I try to listen without it being obvious how much I want to hear what they're saying. My heart misses a beat when I hear my boss's name and the phrase "under federal investigation." Worse, the Feds are seeking him for questioning. I feel the blood drain out of my face and my thoughts running away when Rob and Adriana put another shot in front of me. I down it and head for the men's room.

I return and tell them I need to leave. Adriana looks at me with mysterious eyes and tells me she expects an early departure only if a lady is involved. I smile. She and Rob don't suspect a thing.

As I'm riding back to South Breeze, my mind is racing. I need more information.

Fortunately, I have my laptop. I dig around on the internet and make some unwelcome discoveries.

According to the news stories coming out of Newark, New Jersey (location of Thrift Bank Mortgage's home office), this investigation has been ongoing for a while. When the mortgage meltdown accelerated in the spring of 2008, a lot of complaints surfaced about Thrift Bank, placing them high on the investigation list.

In retrospect, I should have known. Since selling our loans had become nearly impossible, our business began to dry up rapidly. The mortgage guidelines were tightening almost daily, which was causing our volume to drop. Layoffs ensued, increasing my workload. I was an underwriter who had a knack for getting loans processed quickly and efficiently. I had the ability to negotiate with appraisers, closers, real estate agents and brokers to fix problems and close transactions. In a poor environment, it kept me working. My bloated ego let me believe I was that good. But looking back, my negotiating skills were allowing bad loans to close and be sold. The corporate office was burying me in paperwork so they could stay in business. According to news reports, they were sending fictitious files to selected underwriters. When the appraisals came in low, we would pressure the appraisers, forcing them to inflate the value high enough to provide cash back on the transaction. I can't help but wonder how many underwriters were duped into doing exactly what I did.

This story is almost unbelievable, except I'm living it—and likely in a lot of trouble. Ironically, the news reported that wiretaps had picked up on the missing files out of the Jacksonville office. Those recordings triggered the raid on Thrift Bank offices around the country.

I sit back in my room, unsure of whether to laugh or cry about the whole fucked-up mess. My dramatic departure ultimately brought down the house and only because, out of spite, I took a bunch of files. Funnier still, the files are somewhere near Boca Chica Key. One of Florida's chain gangs has probably disposed of them by now. I'm guessing the search is on for me because the Feds will think the files contained evidence. The thing is, they probably did.

Feeling the effects of the shots I had with Rob, I turn the TV to Fox and hole up for the night. I fear my picture could end up on TV but hope I'm just a small piece of this whole thing. One thing is sure—people are looking for me and I'm going to need a friend. The trouble is, my list of friends is very short.

CHAPTER 6

September 10, 2008 7:00 a.m.

I sleep fitfully, so the night passes slowly. Finally I get up, but am fearful of leaving the room. I need coffee, so I cross the street and grab a cup from Ana's Cuban Cafe. I sit down and begin thinking of all the shit I dealt with over the years I was employed at Thrift Bank. I was the consummate professional. I rarely took vacations, and when I did, I stayed connected by computer or Blackberry. I severed nearly all ties with friends. My work days were long, so I had little time to socialize—especially during the boom years from 2003 to 2007. My sister passed away in 2007. It was the only year I hadn't gone to visit her. I still haven't forgiven myself for that. She was a true confidant and I'd give anything to have her with me now.

All morning I sit and watch the news. CNBC woke up to the story, and now it's all over cable. It's another in a series of high-profile fraud cases since the Bernie Madoff scandal broke. The news channels are eating it up. So far, I've heard nothing about me personally.

As I sit and contemplate my next move, reality settles in. I've amassed nearly a million dollars in assets, enough for me to retire. But this investigation could leave me penniless. I always felt like my bonuses were excessive. Now I know why. The large amounts of money kept me working without asking questions. Management didn't need to let me in on their secret as long as I kept signing off on files with no knowledge of wrongdoing. Money kept me quiet. I was a high-dollar pawn. And what sickens me most is that I gave up the better part of my working life for money that may well disappear without me spending a dime of it. If my accounts aren't currently frozen, they soon will be.

Even though Gavin hadn't asked me for identification, I checked in under my real name. I had no reason not to. Worse, I told him exactly who I was when we met the night of the scuffle out front. If I was going to buy time I would need to either check out immediately and leave the island, or level with Gavin, ask for his help and hope for the best. I believe he'd tell me if he wasn't comfortable helping. At least I'd be able to move on to another location.

Around noon I head for the office. I approach Gavin cautiously. "Gavin," I say, "I'm concerned someone may be looking for me. I checked in under my real name and it's very important that I not be found, at least for a while." I continue, "I know this is a strange request, but I'll provide whatever information you need." With a stressed tone in my voice I finish by saying, "God, I'm really hoping you can work with me on this."

He immediately asks, "What do you plan to do with the truck? It sticks out like a sore thumb in the parking lot and if it doesn't disappear, anyone looking for you will know you're here."

I'm relieved, it sounds like he's willing to help. "I don't know," I answer, "but I'm open for suggestions." Then he asks me who we're dealing with; he wants to know what he's up against. I tell him, "Federal officials and possibly the people I used to work for."

He pauses and says, "The truck's gotta go to a chop shop."

I say, "OK, you have any place in mind?"

"I'll knock on your door shortly," he says walking away.

About an hour later, Gavin is at my door. I let him in. He looks me square in the eye and tells me he made a call to a friend in Miami, and they'll be expecting my truck sometime tonight. They'll give me two hundred bucks for it. He gives me directions to the place; it's somewhere in Hialeah. He says Rob will follow and bring me back to Key West. He says to be ready just after dark. He also removed me from the motel records.

On his way out the door he tells me to relax, and believe it or not, I just caught my first break. Under the circumstances, I find this perplexing.

CHAPTER 7

September 10, 2008 2:00 p.m.

It's nearly five hours until dark so I walk across the street and pick up a sandwich at Ana's. I take it back to my room, turn on the TV and hole up again. I feel sick from stress but force myself to eat.

CNBC keeps replaying the story with no change in details. At least for now my name has not been released. I take some comfort in that. I shut off the TV.

I decide to use a technique that served me well in the corporate world when I felt overwhelmed. I begin making a list of things I need to do in order to effect the outcome I desire. My first objective is to stay out of jail. Second, keep my assets. I didn't knowingly break the law. I shouldn't be subject to jail time or asset forfeiture. If the Feds want anything from me, a guarantee on both items will be mandatory. Otherwise, why should I help?

It seems I can stay here in Key West for now. That may give me time to work through this mess. I figure if Gavin or Rob rat me out, I'm in no worse shape than getting apprehended. I can't hide without help, so at least I have a chance. I need leverage, and the files I tossed near Boca Chica are my best option. No one has any idea where they are, including me. I need to find out if there's anything left of them. But how? The likelihood of anything legible being found is probably slim. If I could find something, at least I could prove what I'd done with them. I decide to write down in detail all of the deals that seemed odd to me. Some of that information may be on my laptop. It dawns on me that my computer might be a valuable bargaining chip in the investigation.

I'm really concerned about my Blackberry. I need to get information out of it but am fearful of turning it on. I turned it on the morning after I arrived and if anyone was tracking me then, they'll know I'm here. Since the offices hadn't been raided by then, I'm probably OK. I decide to discuss this with Gavin. Maybe he'll have a suggestion.

Late in the afternoon, Gavin knocks on my door. He enters and sits down on the only chair in the room. I sit on the edge of the bed and he begins asking me questions. First, he asks if I've been using credit cards in my travels. I tell him no. I've always been a cash-and-carry guy. It's something my dad always did, and it rubbed off on me. I tell him carrying cash is why I paid him for two weeks at the motel. It lessens my loss if I get ripped off. He seems pleased and laughs at my reasoning.

I tell him my issue with the Blackberry. He agrees it can't be turned on again. Like me, he's concerned that I turned it on the day after I arrived. He tells me to get all of the information off of it while I'm in Miami tonight, to do it near Bayside Marina and then toss it on a boat headed north on the Intracoastal. If the Feds are watching, they'll head in the wrong direction. He tells me he'll pick up a few pre-paid cell phones for the three of us to communicate. Then I proceed to tell him about the files I tossed out on U.S. 1. I don't think I've heard anyone laugh like that in years. It was contagious because I was surprised to find myself laughing along with him. We decide it would be wise to stop in the area on the way back from Miami. A casual look around shouldn't raise any suspicions.

Before leaving, he asks if I have any other immediate needs. I tell him no, then ask why he's helping me. He smiles and says he has a soft spot for corporate criminals. We both get a laugh out of that one.

CHAPTER 8

September 10, 2008 5:00 p.m.

Rob and I plan to leave in a couple of hours, so I continue working on my list. Waiting is hard, and I begin to realize I'll be doing a lot of it in the coming weeks, possibly months. I decide to hit the ATM a couple of times in Miami. I can find out if my checking account is frozen. If not, I can pick up some extra cash.

I begin to wonder why Gavin and Rob are helping me. No real explanation comes to mind. I haven't told them about my money. If they did know, their motives would be easier to understand. Considering Rob's experience with authority, he might just want to help anyone in the Feds' gun sights. As for Gavin, I don't know. He's been here for a long time. I suspect he's got a history, but would it cause him to help someone he barely knows? Everyone I've ever met has a motive—figuring it out is the challenge. I've heard of altruistic people who do nice things for people and expect nothing in return, but I've never met one. I hope to get more insight on Rob when we drive back to Key West later tonight. For now I sit, wait, and hope.

Rob and Gavin knock on my door early in the evening with cell phones and directions to Dolphin Salvage Yard in Hialeah. A guy named Alvarez runs the place and he'll be expecting me before midnight. The pre-paid cell phones will allow us to communicate with little risk of being tracked once we toss them. He gives Rob and me explicit instructions to only call each other and no one else.

I spend a few minutes cleaning out my truck before departing. I leave my country mix tape in the cassette deck for one last trip down memory lane. I get pissed thinking about the good times I've had in my truck. Such a drastic measure really sucks, driving home the serious nature of what's happening.

I'm ready to go, and Rob informs me he'll be trailing me by about ten minutes. He instructs me to call him from Stock Island. That'll be his cue to leave. I agree and start the truck, and a few seconds later I'm on Simonton Street headed for US 1.

It's the first time I've been off the island since I arrived. A chill runs down my spine when I see a sign indicating north. I offer a secret prayer to whoever is listening that I make it back as planned. As instructed, I call Rob when I reach Stock Island. He departs—which is comforting. At least I know I have backup close behind. It's dark now and the beautiful vistas of the Lower Keys are invisible, which depresses me.

The drive becomes monotonous until I cross the Seven-Mile Bridge. I get a glimpse of a brilliant moonrise over the Atlantic. It's a full moon that lights the sky as bright as day. I've never seen a more beautiful moonrise in my life. Seeing it makes me thankful for the night drive. I slow the vehicle to a crawl, trying to stretch the moment as long as possible. I begin thinking about my life and become overwhelmed with regret. I realize how alone I am.

Two days ago, I was beginning to think about my future. Thinking about life without the duress of deadlines and pushy people. The skies were beginning to look a little sunnier to me. And then, out of nowhere comes this mess.

I want to move forward, but with the past knocking at my door, I can't. My eyes water a bit which makes me realize I'm experiencing a kind of stress I've never encountered. After a few minutes I'm across the bridge and nearing Marathon Key. I begin to compose myself and mentally prepare for the long night ahead.

The phone rings. It's Rob. He's checking to see if he's maintaining a ten-minute tail. He is, and we decide to touch base again when I get to the Hialeah exit on I-95.

CHAPTER 9

September 10, 2008 9:30 p.m.

I pass through Key Largo and begin looking for the left turn that takes me to I-95. My palms begin to sweat, thinking about all I need to accomplish on this trip. Luckily, the traffic's light heading through Florida City, and before long I'm at the Hialeah exit. It's 9:30 p.m. and I'm on schedule—so far.

I call Rob and check his whereabouts. He's close, so I continue weaving through an area of rundown warehouses en route to an industrial area housing the freight yards of CSX Railroad. The Dolphin Salvage Yard sits adjacent to it on a five-acre tract of oil-laden sand. When I pull up to the gate, a heavy-set Cuban guy with a bald head and a goatee approaches. I ask for Alvarez and he points me toward the office. I pop out my country music mix tape, put it in my shirt pocket, and walk toward the office. I open the door and an unkempt, mangy-looking German shepherd lunges at me. Alvarez smirks as he calls off the dog. I tell him I'm delivering a truck. He says he's been expecting me and hands over an envelope. I give him the keys but don't bother paying much attention to the envelope. Under the circumstances I wouldn't care if I got nothing for the truck. I nervously walk out of the office, turn to my left and begin the three-block walk to my rendezvous with Rob. I walk next to a fence surrounding the salvage yard and the dogs inside follow me, growling the whole way. When I reach the corner, I'm relieved to see Rob waiting in his beat-up old CJ-7 Jeep.

I hop in the Jeep, and Rob asks me how I'm doing. I tell him I want my truck back. He just shrugs. I call Gavin and update him. Rob begins weaving his way out of Hialeah en route to Bayside.

We arrive and park on N.E. 3rd Street. It's late, so the meter readers have gone home for the night, lessening our chances of encountering anyone in uniform. We fill the meter with quarters just in case. I remove the backpack with my laptop and Blackberry in it, and we begin walking toward the marina. Rob plans to nose around and find a suitable boat. When he has a good candidate, he'll report back to me. Then I'll turn on the Blackberry, check the messages and sync it with the computer before Rob gets it on a northbound boat.

It's 11:30 p.m. when Rob returns out of breath, telling me he found a boat. It's currently refueling and will be pulling out in approximately forty-five minutes. But there's a problem. It's headed to the Bahamas. I think about it for a minute and decide to call Gavin. He tells me to go ahead and use it. It might even complicate matters more for the Feds. I wait another ten minutes, and with some trepidation, finally turn on the Blackberry.

It lights up and when I see it has a signal, I know the clock is ticking. I don't know how long it will take for anyone to pinpoint my location. I'm hoping a minimum of thirty minutes. As long as none of the voice mail messages are long-winded, I should be OK.

I already have the computer booted up when I turn on the Blackberry, so syncing the two takes less than five minutes. I now have all of my business and personal contacts saved in the computer. Step #1 complete.

I dial into voice mail and find twelve messages. The first is from Brett Bowers, a Thrift Bank underwriter in Trenton, New Jersey. We became work friends at a conference a couple of years back. He left me his number and tells me he needs to talk with me soon. He leaves his home number. The next is from my former boss, John. He's still really pissed but seems genuinely scared. He leaves all of his numbers. I enjoy the fear in his tone. I'm not sure if he's involved or fearing his superiors. Either way, I don't care about his problems. The third is from a guy named Don Opitz, whom I've never met. He's a high-level player from the home office in Newark. He demands the files. He leaves a cell number and tells me it's in my best interest to call. I'm baffled about what the hell was in those files and why everyone is hell bent on finding them. Next, I get a little comic relief when Nikki rants again about all of this mess being my fault. Did she not think this house of cards was going to fall at some point anyway? She didn't bother to leave a number.

The next message sends a nasty chill through me. It's a federal agent named Dave Friedly. He leaves a return number and says if he hasn't heard from me in two days, a warrant will be issued for my arrest. The deadline has already passed.

I begin to well up again when I hear my old buddy Arthur's voice checking to see if I'm OK. He's the one buddy from my childhood who always managed to stay in touch. We haven't spoken in a couple of years, but he's always been one of my closest friends. He leaves a number and tells me to call anytime.

The last call is from Lindsey, the sexy little vixen who manages my condo complex. She tells me that my door was kicked in and the place was ransacked. She had one of the maintenance guys secure it but wants to talk with me.

The rest of the messages are unrelated to recent events—just clueless clients wanting to know about their loans.

It takes me a total of twenty minutes to finish my work. I signal Rob and he takes the phone and heads for the dock. I shut down the computer, pack it up, and head toward Third Street. I stop at the Bank of America ATM on the way and hit it for three hundred dollars. Fortunately it works, which means the feds haven't frozen my account yet. I decide not to visit any more ATM machines. I've got enough money and don't want to put Rob at additional risk. Further, I hadn't discussed this with Gavin.

When I get to the car I wait in the shadows under a tree for about 10 minutes until Rob returns. We head for I-95, and before long we're on U.S. 1 passing through Kendall. We begin to relax a little. Rob tells me the phone is on a big boat with a bunch of rich guys having a bachelor party. He says there's a couple of smoking-hot party girls accompanying them. We crack up at the thought of customs and the Bahamian authorities giving them a warm welcoming party when they arrive in Bimini. Sadly, we'll probably never find out.

It's 1 a.m. when we check in with Gavin. We're on schedule and should be at Boca Chica Channel around 3:30 a.m. Gavin is pleased. We should be home by daybreak just as planned.

Rob and I talk a lot the next couple of hours. He's one of those guys you meet who really doesn't give a shit about anything most people find important. If he doesn't want to do something or be around someone, he just says no. He doesn't care about making a lot of money. He's clear about that. He believes money comes if you're not chasing it. He cares more about enjoying his life and taking care of people close to him. He says in life, what else do we really have? It's the smartest thing I've heard him say. I decide that a couple of years in prison would probably make anyone philosophical. A year or two ago I would have thought his thinking was ludicrous. Today it makes perfect sense.

It's nearly 4 a.m. when we arrive at the area where I began tossing the files out the window. Rob pulls the Jeep over, and out of nowhere a police car with lights flashing moves in behind us. I'm panicky but Rob is calm and tells me to relax. He says they look for drunks out here every night and this is no more than a routine stop. I'm sweating bullets as the officer approaches. He asks Rob for his license and registration. Rob complies and the officer asks what we're doing here. Rob coolly tells him we're looking for a place to fish. The officer then asks if we've been drinking. Rob answers no. Within a few minutes the officer returns and tells us the fish have been biting near the bridge in the early morning hours. He tells us we're free to go. Rob thanks him, pulls forward, gets out of the jeep and pulls a bunch of fishing gear out of the rear storage compartment. He looks at me and smiles. He says the fishing gear gives us a perfect reason to be nosing around out here at this time of the night. I sigh and smirk, realizing what Gavin told me about Rob is dead on. He's smart. Needing cover was the last thing on my mind.

We set up a couple of poles at the water's edge and begin scouring the areas where I tossed the files. I walk around finding pieces of the documents—a page here and a page there. Rob has about the same luck. We eagerly pick up everything we can, hoping it will somehow help. We hit pay dirt when we find a manila folder thick with papers. How it survived I'll never know. They're rain soaked and stuck together from the weather, but at least we have something. The sun is beginning to rise off to the east and we know it's time to go. We put the papers in plastic trash bags, throw them in the back seat and continue toward Key West. It's about 6:30 a.m. when we turn left onto Simonton from U.S. 1. When we pull into the South Breeze, Rob opens the door and I retrieve the trash bags. I thank him and he tells me we'll talk soon. Gavin approaches and tells us both to get some rest.

I walk into my room, toss the bag, crank up the A.C. and collapse on the bed.

CHAPTER 10

September 11, 2008 10:15 a.m.

The pounding on my door would have woken a hibernating bear. I hear Gavin yelling at me to open the door, as I'm stumbling around the room trying to figure out what's going on. I open it, and Gavin bursts in telling me to get packed. He says I'm leaving for a while and turns on the TV. I grab the remote and turn the channel to Fox News. He tells me to pack while I'm watching. It's only been five hours since I returned from Miami, I've had very little sleep, and I'm confused—really confused. He asks me about a guy named John Marris. I tell him he's my former boss, and ask him how the hell he knew that. He tells me John is dead. He was found in Miami last night. Further, he informs me that my picture is on the news as a person of interest in his death. All of the news channels are running the story.

As the news sinks in, I'm overcome by a wave of emotions: shock, fear, and anger. I start screaming every curse word I've ever known, throwing things and punching the walls. I throw the remote at the TV and it shatters into pieces. Gavin grabs me and holds me in a bear hug trying to calm me down. I relax a bit and sit at the edge of the bed for a few minutes. As the wave passes, there's an unfamiliar hollow feeling in my stomach. Gavin begins packing my things and tells me he has a place for me to go.

It's twenty minutes later when we load up Gavin's old Pontiac with all of my stuff. We pull onto Simonton Street and wind our way around to Roosevelt Boulevard headed to the far end of Smather's Beach.

On our way to Smather's, Gavin tells me we're leaving for Ballast Key, fourteen miles from Key West. It's a 26-acre island with only three houses. The owner is a real-estate developer from New York who rarely visits. I'm to be the new caretaker.

I ask about the owner coming in unexpectedly. Gavin says he likes his privacy, so he always calls ahead to have the caretaker clear out before he arrives. Gavin met the owner years ago when he stayed at the South Breeze. They struck up a friendship, and when he bought the island, he hired Gavin to handle the upkeep and maintenance. When Gavin has no one to stay on the island, he has Rob visit a couple of times a week to check on it. Luckily for me, it's been vacant for a month.

Rob is waiting with a flats-boat when we arrive at Smather's. The place is deserted, so no one sees us as we toss my stuff in. Gavin shakes my hand, then pulls me close and embraces me. He tells me Rob will get me squared away when we get to the island, and that they'll both be out to see me in a couple of days. He says we have a lot to talk about and he'll plan on staying the night.

Rob fires the engine, and we back out from the beach to begin our journey. Smather's is on the opposite side of Key West from Ballast Key, but Rob and Gavin chose to bring me here for departure instead of taking the risk of leaving from Key West Harbor. With my picture all over the news, it's important that I not be seen. Rob's flats-boat moves awkwardly through the open water. Since a flats-boat is built for moving through shallow water at a low speed, I'm perplexed. We have fourteen miles to navigate and it's clearly not built for this trip. I ask him why he chose to use it. He says, "I'll understand when we get there." He also informs me of his plan to cook some fish when we get there, and we have to catch them on the way. Since I have nothing else to do, it seems like a fine idea.

After a while, we slow to trolling speed. Rob baits a couple of hooks, sets up two poles, and we putt along hoping for a bite. It doesn't take long, and we catch a couple of red snapper. Rob's pleased, so we put away the fishing gear and continue on towards Ballast. Every time I get quiet, Rob starts talking again, trying to keep me from sinking too deeply into my thoughts. I play along, knowing I'll have plenty of time alone soon.

We motor across glassy, clear water until finally, Ballast Key comes into view. The island is larger than I thought, with beautiful beaches lined with lush palms. We approach from the east, which allows us a perfect view of the sprawling 500-foot walkway to the only boat dock on the island. Rob points it out and tells me if I ever see a boat there without a notice from him or Gavin, stay out of sight. He continues past the dock, showing me other areas of the island, when suddenly he turns inward toward a low-water marshy area. He throttles the engine up and beaches the boat under a camouflage canopy between two trees near the caretaker's house. He winks at me, and I immediately understand why we rode in the flats-boat. The walk to my quarters is no more than twenty-five yards. Better yet, the boat can't be seen from the water or the air.

I begin unloading the boat, still in a daze from all that's happened in the last couple of days. Fortunately Rob had made a trip to the store for some much needed supplies. I make several trips to the front porch, leaving each item until the boat is empty.

We're finally unloaded when Rob inserts his key and opens the door.

The house is small and quaint, charming even. The front door opens into a combination kitchen and living room. It's furnished with island-style bamboo chairs and a matching coffee table. The bedroom and bathroom are in the back of the place through a short hallway. A small laundry room with a computer desk is across the hall from the bathroom. Fishing charts hang on the wall along with an aviation chart of the Keys. The floors are stone with area rugs spread throughout. The place feels comfortable. I begin to feel myself relax.

After I arrange my things in the house, I walk out on the porch and am taken by the view. Crystal-clear Caribbean waters shine as far as the eye can see. The porch has an outdoor flowered couch with a matching chair. Next to the chair is a tile table with a seashell setting on the top. I realize if I'm going to be hiding somewhere, there's no better place. The trouble is, this extended vacation might get really boring after a while. I've got to figure a way out of this mess.

Rob is messing around in the back of the house when all of a sudden I hear the sound of a gas-powered motor firing up. He walks around the corner and motions me to the back, where a generator sits. He says I have enough fuel to run the generator for approximately three hours a day. He'll be making a trip to the island every three to four days to bring supplies and check on me. He waves me back inside the house and shows me a satellite dish and a small TV. He also shows me the Internet connection and asks me for my computer. Within a few minutes he has me configured and a connection established. He then takes me to the bedroom closet and shows me something that looks like a base station CB radio. He explains to me that it's a single side band amateur radio transceiver, and gives me the call sign and frequency information for Gavin at the South Breeze. Twice daily I'm instructed to check in on it. The rest of my communication is to be done by e-mail. Rob gives me a Yahoo email address. He will check it twice daily from various locations around Key West. He'll take care of any phone calls or legwork I need done. He then looks at me and says, "Enough of this bullshit for now." He opens his cooler, throws me a beer, pulls out a bottle of tequila and pours us a shot. We down the shot and head to the porch with the beers. The house faces east so the sun sets behind us, affording cool, shaded evenings. Rob says he much prefers the sunrises from this porch. I look at him and ask how many he's seen from here. "Plenty," he says. It dawns on me that Rob has hidden here too.

One beer leads to another, and a short while later Rob begins showing me how to use the rudimentary kitchen. It has a propane oven/stove combo unit and a microwave. A fresh water tank feeds the main house. It usually needs a fill twice a year. A small frigate comes in from Key West Harbor whenever it runs low. The icebox only runs when the generator is on, so everything goes from frozen to thawed regularly. He tells me the fuller it's kept, the better it works. Keeping a line in the water will usually keep plenty of fish in the freezer. He smirks and tells me he hopes I like fish. He says I probably won't by the time I leave.

Around the back of the house is a small storage area. It houses a grill, a bicycle, and various hand tools. It also has a chainsaw, a brush hog, and gas-powered weed eaters. Rob breaks out the grill and tells me we'll go through the tools and the chore list in the morning. It's the first I knew of him staying overnight. I'm glad. Strangely, I really didn't want to spend my first night here alone.

Rob pulls the two red snapper out of the boat and begins cleaning them. He packages what we don't need in freezer bags and puts it away. We both work in the kitchen getting the food and utensils situated. We fire up the grill and manage to make a delicious meal.

Clean-up is easy, considering the disposable dishware. Water conservation is more important than trash concerns, which suits me. We take all the trash behind the house and put it in a metal drum. Rob suggests burning it every four to five days. He instructs me to do it at night so boats can't see the smoke. He suggests staying out of sight as much as possible. On occasion, he informs me, boaters come into Key West Harbor and ask questions about the island, and it's better if the questions don't include smoke and fires.

With dinner complete, we sit on the porch, watch the moon rise over the Atlantic, and finish the beers Rob brought. Our conversation veers into some detail about Rob's troubles with the law. It turns out he had to hide here after being freed on bail. The people he was smuggling for were trying to kill him because they thought he would turn state's evidence, and the feds wanted to put him away for life due to the amount of pot he was carrying. As it worked out, one of the men in the smuggling ring was the son of the Bahamian president, and Rob threatened to go public with that information. It was a ploy. He tells me it was the only card he had to play.

If it hadn't worked, he was prepared to leave the island for South America and live on the run. He said his bosses would have killed him. Turning them in was not an option.

The U.S. State Department and Bahamian officials were working closely on drug interdiction at the time, which was really unpopular in the Bahamas. Even the perception of impropriety within the Bahamian government would have upset the balance of power in the Bahamas and could have shut down the interdiction efforts.

Ultimately, the Feds felt the risk was too big and they elected to give Rob two years in a Dade County correctional facility followed by ten years probation. It took him six months to work out his deal. He did it all in hiding—right here on Ballast Key. His disdain for the government is evident.

It's getting late and we're really drunk by the time Rob takes me inside and shows me how to operate the fans. They're on battery power and he suggests running them only at night. They're hooked to marine batteries and automatically recharge when the generator runs. I thank him for everything. He walks into the main living area, makes up a bed on the couch, and says goodnight. I walk into the bedroom and pass out.

CHAPTER 11

September 12, 2008 11:00 a.m.

The early morning sun has already given way to the afternoon heat by the time Rob and I begin to move around. We brew a pot of coffee and enjoy a couple of rolls and fresh fruit. We finish, and Rob tells me to follow him. He begins showing me the rest of the island. We walk on a cleared path lined with coral rocks until we arrive at the main house. It's a bungalow-style cottage with a large wrap-around porch. The roof is metal, and the siding is the color of stone. Palm trees fill the yard, adding to the oasis feel of the island. When we get to the front door, Rob enters and shows me around. The house is much larger than it looks from the outside. The furniture is modest. Seashells, beach paintings, and a flamingo statue bring the island feel into the house. The front of the house faces the beach, directly south. The rear has a view of the finely manicured backyard, and just beyond a verdant, peaceful lagoon. Rob says he's caught a lot of fish there.

We walk around the entire house. Rob tells me to run a little water through the pipes every two or three days and flush the toilets at least as often. He shows me several areas outside to check for pests.

We head back to the caretaker house where Rob explains my duties, using a list that hangs on the back of the shed door. Most of the work is in the backyard of the main house. Other than that, my role is to keep an eye on things. Rob tells me he only worked a few hours a day while he was here and the place looked immaculate. He says the work was a welcome respite from all that was happening around him.

Rob finishes giving me instructions and says it's time for him to leave. He tells me to check in with Gavin on the radio at noon and 6 p.m. every day. I agree and walk him over to the boat. He gives me a thumbs-up sign as he backs out the boat to return to Key West. He yells that he'll see me tomorrow evening and Gavin will be with him. I motion thumbs-up and wave goodbye.

As I walk back to my quarters, I pause for a moment to enjoy the view, the heat, and knowing I have some time to gather my thoughts.

The document-filled trash bags are the first thing I begin looking through when I return to the house. A lot of the papers are wet. Slowly and laboriously, I pull apart pages that have stuck together, and I lay them out to dry. As I'm doing this, I notice nothing odd or out of place. But I hope that over the days and weeks to come, something begins to lead me closer to an answer as to why these pieces of paper have become so much a part of this nightmare.

I step out back and fire up the generator. I need to log onto the Internet and check the news. After a few minutes, the TV is on and the computer is up and running. Nothing new is being reported. I set up a new Google email address and send a test email to the address Rob gave me yesterday. I search through the old client files I saved on my hard drive. I never had any real use for this information, but for some reason I felt the need to have it with me. For the first time, I recognize the absurdity of it all—the illusion of always having control, and being able to solve problems from anywhere at anytime. Those files might actually be useful now, just not in the way I had originally thought.

After a couple of hours of digging through the computer files, the only things that seem to be worthy of further investigation are the larger commercial deals that were beginning to come across my desk during the last eighteen months. The deals were larger than most I had done in the previous years. Moreover, they were more complicated. We would have first, second, and sometimes third mortgages on them. The appraisal values were stratospheric but the underwriting guidelines were usually less stringent. The investors purchasing the loans were large hedge funds from money centers around the world. They understood the business risk involved and didn't seem to mind taking it. In retrospect, perhaps they didn't understand the risk so well after all.

I shut the generator down in time to leave enough fuel for a few minutes of TV and a radio call to Gavin this evening. I've had my fill of reviewing files and decide to head out and explore the island on my own. Ballast Key is long and narrow, and it doesn't take long to explore all of it. The beaches are not as nice on the far side, making it evident why the houses are placed where they are. It's a strange feeling to be on an island by myself—strangely pleasant.

I return in time to check in with Gavin, so I get the generator going and turn on the radio. Our communication is limited because it's not secure. We simply say hello and exchange pleasantries. That's the code for things being OK. I check Gmail and find Rob has responded to my test email. I'm all set up on the island. Now I just need to figure out how in the hell I'm going to get out of here.

After cooking some of last night's leftover fish, I down a shot of tequila and savor the intense burn. I toss a line in the water and sit on the porch enjoying the view. The files are still whirling around in my head when it dawns on me that I need to contact that underwriter from Trenton, New Jersey. I can't help wondering if he's in as much trouble as I am. He may have useful information. The trouble is, he could be under surveillance or, worse yet, working with the Feds or this Don Opitz guy from Newark.

While waiting for the fishing pole to announce the arrival of my next meal, my mind wanders back to my interactions with John, my former boss. Why would he be dead? Was it suicide? But it's too much of a coincidence for him to pull that trigger in Miami while I was there. Strangely, I don't feel sorry for him. He was a prick, plain and simple. But I question whether he's the kind of guy who would have been involved in this. He made a lot of trips to the home office and seemed very close to upper management, but he didn't seem high enough in the organization to be directly involved. It's possible he knew just enough to get him killed. And the fact that he was knocked off in Miami while I was there could certainly mean that whoever killed him wanted the Feds coming after me. But how did his killers know I was in Miami? Is it possible that someone inside the government is tied to Thrift Bank Mortgage? I decide to try and do a thorough investigation of Thrift Bank Mortgage—but not until tomorrow.

I spend a few minutes carefully piling up the documents I laid out this morning. They're crinkled and stiff but otherwise legible. With a little luck, I'll be able to glean some information from them at some point.

After dark, I light a kerosene lamp and begin making a list of things I need, including at least three external hard drives. It's crucial that I back up the files on my computer. Rounding out my list is a printer, paper, file folders, standard office supplies, and beer. With Rob and Gavin coming to visit tomorrow, I decide to send Rob an email first thing in the morning.

CHAPTER 12

September 13, 2008 6:00 a.m.

It's not quite daybreak when I hear the sound of a rooster crowing in front of the house. It pisses me off. I cover my ears with the extra pillow and pray it leaves—no luck. After another twenty minutes, I give up trying to sleep, start the generator, email Rob my list, and brew some fresh coffee.

The day passes slowly as I wait for Rob and Gavin to arrive. During our noon radio talk, Gavin says to look for them around 4 o'clock—as if I might have plans to be out. I spend the early part of the afternoon making a few notes on issues to discuss with them. When I head to the porch to wait, my fishing pole is bent over and shaking slightly. I reel it in and find a small red-fish. Rob was right. It didn't take much effort, just a little time. I clean it and place it in the freezer.

Rob and Gavin arrive late. My anxiety level rises with each passing minute when finally I see them motoring in from the horizon. In this moment I realize how dependent I am on their help, and that without it I'd already be in jail. I don't even have to ask why they're late. It's as if Rob already knew I'd be worried when he yells, " Sorry, Petey, traffic on the island was a nightmare today."

They have everything I asked for and more. All of the fixings for a huge dinner. We talk as we cook. I sense Gavin is holding something back, but I'm so hungry I don't make it a point to ask. A real dinner hits the spot with steak, garlic bread, baked potato and fresh salad. After dinner Gavin opens a bottle of scotch and pours us all a shot.

We retire to the porch and discuss the events of the last few days. Gavin looks me in the eye and sternly demands complete honesty and candor about all the details surrounding the trouble I'm facing. He tells me he understands how difficult this situation is because he was in trouble once, many years ago and had to hide for a while. It took him a few months to sort things out, and the result was a new life in Key West. It's the first time he's mentioned his past to me. I suspected he had a colorful past—now I know.

I start by telling him and Rob about the voicemail messages I received when we were in Miami. We went over each one in detail. They're both interested in the one John left for me. Unfortunately, I didn't note the time and date stamp so we can't be sure when it came in. The call from Brett Bowers, the underwriter in Trenton, also interests them. They agree with me that calling him could be a trap—but it might be worth it. They joke about the message from Nikki, but they feel strongly about contacting her too, in spite of how I left things. We're all in agreement that I not call anyone from Thrift Bank or the Fed. At this point, we just don't have enough information.

The conversation continues late into the night. All of us agree that this is almost certainly a big case—especially since my boss ended up dead in Miami while I was there. At this point, I tell them about my stop at the ATM. I apologize and tell them I had no idea how big this mess was going to be. Gavin's eyes light up when he hears this. Suddenly, it makes sense to me as well. It's likely that my employers tracked me through the ATM, and the Feds through both the ATM and the cell phone. Since Thrift Bank has access to bank records, they easily would have flagged my account. When they discovered my whereabouts, they took John to Miami and killed him, leaving suspicion to fall on me because of the workplace issues we had in Jacksonville. One thing is sure: John winding up dead in Miami is not a coincidence. And we all agree that it's also possible someone with the Feds could have leaked the information to Thrift Bank officials, which would mean someone within the government is involved. But how? We all agree that no one can be trusted yet.

Gavin and Rob question me about my motivation in all of this. They want to know what I'm protecting. They ask how I feel about possible jail time, living on the run, or losing all I've worked for in lieu of jail time. The questions are tough, but I've had enough time to think them through. I've been asking myself the same questions. I decide they need to know everything. Over the next couple of hours I go into detail about the money I've saved and invested over the years, and how I gave away my youth and abandoned my dreams to work long hours in the corporate hotbox so someday I could quit and live the "good life." My story is familiar to them as they both had a similar mindset at some point in their lives. I tell them I'd trade the money for no jail time. I'll only live on the run if someone's trying to kill me. If I must do time, it must be short and I want the best deal I can get. I'll give the Feds what I have only if I feel they're being fair and only if I trust them. We all agree that protecting Thrift Bank should not be a concern. I wasn't a knowing part of the illegal enterprise. I played a part in it, so I could be deemed involved; but protecting something I unwittingly participated in is not my concern.

Gavin and Rob begin discussing techniques for communicating that won't reveal my location. They begin brainstorming about ways to find out if someone in the government is working with Thrift Bank officials. If so, my problem is much worse. The only idea they have is to set up a meeting, use me as bait, and see who shows up. While they don't have a plan yet, they decide to formulate one over the next few days. They instruct me never to send an email from Ballast to anyone other than Rob in Key West. He will move throughout South Florida sending emails and making calls for me as necessary. They're both concerned about I.P. addresses tied to all computers. Gavin believes a satellite phone will be untraceable for short calls, but wants to verify that assumption before using a contact he has in Miami to get one. Gavin tells me I'm going to need patience because communication is going to be like the Stone Age. I cringe, knowing he's right.

Our last bit of discussion surrounds my activities the first week or so I was in Key West. They both want to know if I made an impression on anyone who might remember me. Rob was already aware of Adriana and told me he didn't think she would be a problem. So far, she hadn't mentioned anything to him. I told them about my tryst with the annoying chick with the grating northeastern accent. She concerns me. When I tell them how I left her, the story provides some much-needed comic relief. I tell them other than that, I blended in as a nice drunk.

The sun is climbing over the horizon and we realize it's too late to go to sleep. Gavin pours the last of our scotch into three glasses, drops in a few pieces of ice, and says, "Enjoy." About that time, the rooster starts crowing out back, and I jump to my feet and run to the rear of the house. Tip-toeing quietly behind it, I lunge, falling to the ground as the cock runs off into the bushes. Rob sees this, doubles over laughing and calls me a dumbass. A minute or two later he comes around the corner with a pellet gun and says to use it instead of breaking my neck.

Exhaustion is setting in as they back the boat out and head for home. We plan to reconvene in a couple of days. Gavin will have the answers regarding the satellite phone, and Rob will make an attempt to contact Brett Bowers in Trenton. Since I gave Rob some details about a convention only Brett and I would know about, we hope he'll open up and give us information that might be helpful.

Once Gavin and Rob are out of sight, I head into the house, lay my head on the pillow and quickly lose consciousness.

CHAPTER 13

September 15, 2008 10:00 a.m.

The next two days pass slowly, with little new information. I receive a couple of short emails from Rob about getting in touch with Brett in Trenton. He succeeded, but Brett didn't offer any information that could shed light on the situation. Maybe he's as much in the dark as I am. Gavin did acquire a satellite phone. He found out it can provide approximately three minutes of talk time before being effectively traced, and if it is traced, it doesn't pin-point an exact location—only the general vicinity.

I'm bored until the time comes for a radio call to Gavin. Fortunately, he tells me Rob will be coming tomorrow and staying overnight. I'm relieved, knowing some information as well as diversion will arrive with him.

It's been nearly four days since I arrived on Ballast. At Rob and Gavin's insistence, I quit shaving and began letting my hair grow out. I've always had the high-and-tight military cut so the growth feels strange. I know at some point I'll have to travel, and altering my appearance can't hurt. My face itches from the unshaven hair. It's not quite a beard, but it's thicker than a five o'clock shadow. Since I've never grown facial hair, I hope what I've been told is true—that the itch goes away soon.

Out of both boredom and necessity, I start researching all of Thrift Bank Mortgage's upper management team. The searches bring up a lot of worthless community service work, charity affiliations, press releases, and an occasional newspaper article about a speech given somewhere. One pattern seems to emerge: a lot of connections to New Jersey Senator Bernie Frankel, including campaign contributions, photos at fund-raisers, and golf outings. The records date back nearly 10 years, and the contributions are for the maximum allowable under federal law. It may mean nothing, but I take note nonetheless.

The generator fuel is running low, so I quickly copy all of my work files onto the external hard drives Rob brought with him a couple of days ago. I use flash drives to copy individual files I think are potentially more important. I make an inventory of file names and copy them to a separate flash drive. I also save my search results on Thrift Bank and print them for official access and review. The flash drives can provide quick access to important information that I can easily keep with me at all times. It occurs to me that I may have to run again, and I don't know if I'll have time to pack.

After nearly three hours of computer work, I shut everything down and head to the main house. The place needs some dusting and a little sweeping so I spend an hour or so tidying it up. Once things are in order, I drop a line in the lagoon to see if I can catch dinner. The old pole I'm using has a hand-tied, artificial lure so I'm not optimistic. I sit, wait, and watch.

I think back to when I became a mortgage underwriter. I was broke. Plain and simple. I'd finished college and was saddled with student loan debt—but I was happy. Being a sucker for adventure, I decided to get my pilot's license. I loved airplanes and had always dreamed of flying for a living. One license led to another, and the next thing I knew, I had doubled my debt load becoming a marketable pilot—only to find out the jobs being offered wouldn't even make the monthly payment on the student loan debt. I've never regretted the efforts I made to fly, only the decision to make a left turn into the mortgage business. I can't help but wonder what would've happened if I had dealt with the low pay at that point in my life. Would I be flying a jet today instead of running from everything and everyone I know? I made the safe and logical choice. But chasing your dreams is the only way to live a fulfilling and creative life. In light of recent events, I clearly made the wrong choice.

The afternoon sun is sliding down the west side of the sky when I decide to head back to my quarters. I brace the pole firmly in the sand, hoping I'll find a nice fish in the morning.

I settle into the couch on the guest house front porch and begin re-reading the files Rob and I had found on U.S. 1. As was the case the first time, nothing stands out. When the daylight disappears, I bait another hook, toss out a line, brace the pole and head to bed. It's not long before the ocean breeze and the sound of the surf lull me into the deepest, uninhibited sleep I've experienced in years.

Nearly ten hours later, that damn cock announces daybreak. Pissed, I go for the pellet gun and take aim. Just as I shoot, the cock leans over, pecking at the ground. Miss! It hears the shot and bolts into the palmetto bushes. Next time, asshole.

The generator hums to life on the first pull, and I head to the kitchen for a pot of coffee. I turn on the computer and begin searching for news about Thrift Bank. The last couple of days revealed very little on the story. I decide to research Bernie Frankel and see what role he plays in the Senate. I'm digging through records when I see something about a finance committee. The lights on the monitor go dim and I hear the CPU fan winding down and realize the generator has shut off. A surge of anger pulsates through me. I quickly write a few notes, cuss the whole fucking mess, and step out on the porch to calm down.

With the fuel supply exhausted, I'm out of electricity until Rob arrives. It's nearly noon, and since it's time to radio Gavin, I hurriedly make the connection changes in order to use battery power for that call. When we chat, I inform him of my fuel situation. He hears the aggravation in my voice and tells me to calm down, everything will arrive soon.

CHAPTER 14

September 15, 2008 4:00 p.m.

It's late in the afternoon when Rob jolts me out of a peaceful nap with his boat horn. He's brought a full load of beer and groceries, and a couple of five-gallon cans of gas. He's as happy and jovial as I've ever seen him. I ask him what he's been smoking. He tells me life is much more exciting since I arrived. I shake my head and say, "I'm glad my predicament is so much fun."

He pats me on the shoulder and says, "Relax, things will work out."

While unloading, our conversation turns to Brett Bowers. Rob made the trip to Tampa and phoned him from there. Since Brett had no idea who Rob was, he told Rob to fuck off—even though Rob knew some things that only I could have told him.

His exact words were: "If Pete needs information, that pussy should call me himself." Rob told Brett he'd pass that along. I chuckle at Rob and tell him he must have one hell of a way with words.

The boat's unloaded and Rob opens a couple beers and hands me one. Then he reaches into his backpack and pulls out a phone. It looks like a cell phone from the 1980s. It's big and cumbersome.

It's the satellite phone Gavin acquired. It's for outbound calls only and it's set automatically to block caller ID. He gives me firm instructions to keep calls under three minutes. He then says I should call Brett this evening.

While we're cooking dinner, I ask Rob about the aviation charts on the laundry room walls. He tells me he used to fly a lot during his days of shuttling boats. He says he loves flying and still does so on occasion, but now only with another pilot. The Feds revoked his license after the smuggling charges. I tell him I also fly, and his eyes light up. Even though I haven't flown in a few years, he's excited to learn I have knowledge and experience with airplanes. He says he has access to a plane, and on occasion gets to fly it to remote airfields in the Keys. We talk aviation, each of us detailing our experience level. My hours of flight time far exceed his. But his bush experience inspires me.

The evening sun begins to fade away when dinner is done. We make a half-assed attempt at cleaning up and then head to the porch to try out the satellite phone. I decide to call Nikki first. I dread calling her. I used her to wreak havoc in the office and get back at her prick husband. She didn't deserve it, and, strangely, I feel a hint of remorse. Nevertheless, I dial her number and wait for an answer. Rob starts a stopwatch and sets it next to me.

She answers. I tell her it's me and that I can only talk for a couple of minutes. She says she knows I didn't kill John but doesn't care if I take the rap. I let her vent for about thirty seconds and then cut her off.

I ask about the last time she saw John. She says three men from New Jersey arrived at their house, and he left with them the night before he was found in Miami. He knew one of them, Don, but not the others. One of the men had blond hair and beady blue eyes, the other was of Hispanic descent. I ask if she would recognize them if I could find a picture. She thinks she could. She then says John had been over-the-edge stressed for about two months before things blew up. Something was going really wrong, but she couldn't figure it out. When I left the office that day, it all began to unravel. The stopwatch goes off. I tell her I'll call again and hang up.

I tell Rob about John and the people from New Jersey. We both feel confident his was a shush murder. His shifty, squirrelly, and generally prickish style didn't exactly endear him to others. He was likely killed because someone thought he knew too much. He probably did, but he probably would have kept quiet. He just never had the ability to convince anyone he was trustworthy.

Rob looks at me and says, "One down, one to go. Time to call Brett. Tell him he can talk to me the next time I call." Rob tells me he's using the name Ty. I smirk and tell him, "OK Ty, I'll take care of that."

I dial Brett Bowers's number. Luckily, he answers. I tell him it's me. The tension is palpable, even over a satellite connection. I ask if he can talk. He says his attorney told him not to, and he thinks his phone could be tapped. After a long pause, I say, "OK." He says, "Good luck, Pete, I'm pulling for you." I hang up and tell Rob exactly what was said.

So maybe Brett does have information he wants to share. We're both sure of it but guess he doesn't want to jeopardize his case. Getting that information is important. Rob and I discuss options for communicating with him. With the information I have, we might be able to help each other. It seems a trip north might be necessary. But communicating through his attorney might be effective as well. I decide to call him back. When I do, he pauses and hesitantly gives me his attorney's name. I thank him and immediately hang up.

Rob and I then discuss Nikki. We agree it's a good bet that the man John knew, Don, is the same man who left a message on my phone. I make a note to search the Internet for a photo of Don Opitz.

Rob decides it's time to step up the drinking, so we pour a shot of tequila and head out back to light the trash barrel. After a few hours of general drunkenness and pyrotechnics, we call it a night.

I wake just before dawn, with a throbbing hangover. Rob doesn't move when I walk through the living area searching for the pellet gun. I find it and grab a jug of water and take a seat on the porch. As I'm waiting, I notice my pole wiggling. I forgot that I left it out two nights ago. After waiting an hour for the no-show cock, I bring in the fish, clean it, and throw it in the icebox. Rob's still out, so I head over to the main house and check the other pole. No fish, so I leave it on the beach and head back to wake Rob.

But first, I walk to the rear of the house, fuel the generator and fire it up. I walk back into the house, and Rob grumbles at me to shut up. I brew some fresh coffee and set a shot of tequila next to his head. It has the desired effect. He nearly pukes, which gets him moving immediately.

We head out to the porch, plop down on the couch and compare our respective hangovers. Undecided about which of us feels worse, we discuss the searches I was working on when I lost power yesterday. Rob, still grumbling about his hangover, agrees to stay while I continue those searches.

I head for the computer and resume my work from yesterday. I pull up the search on Bernie Frankel. After scrolling through a few Google pages, I find the information I was looking at when the power shut off. As I'm reading, a cold chill runs through me. I discover Frankel is the chairman of the Senate Banking Committee. He oversees policies that directly affect Fannie Mae and Freddie Mac, the government-backed mortgage corporations that purchase all FHA loans and a lion's share of conventional loans for the U.S. residential market. I yell at Rob to get his ass in here and take a look at what I've found. He takes a moment to look it over and calmly says I'll be needing more fuel for the generator.

I'm taken aback by the information, and so is Rob. It doesn't incriminate Frankel in any way, but it raises serious questions. I'm not sure what to do next, so Rob and I decide to sit and brainstorm.

It isn't long until noon rolls around. I turn on the radio and check in with Gavin. Rob pipes in, telling Gavin he'll be back to assist him at the motel by evening.

We cook some fish for lunch and continue our discussion about Frankel. We agree that we need more information. We also agree that if, and it's a big if, Frankel is involved in any way, he'll be well insulated from this mess.

Rob starts packing up late in the day for his ride back to Key West. Before he leaves, he tells me he thought his case was complicated until he thinks about the ramifications of mine. He tells me the government involvement in his case was not nearly as deep or potentially as dark as this. He says to keep my chin up, answers will come.

I wave good-bye as he backs the boat out. I head to the porch and begin reading a John Grisham book I'd borrowed from the main house yesterday. I'd rather be immersed in someone else's drama right now.

CHAPTER 15

September 16, 2008 6:00 p.m.

Several hours of reading relaxes me, and my hangover has receded into mild fatigue. I head into the house and radio Gavin. Rob made it back, and all seems well in Key West. I'm too tired to mess with cooking so I pop in a microwave burrito, open a soda and turn on the computer. The Grisham book gave me an idea, so I plan to dig into the Frankel connection further.

I begin searching incorporation records with Bernie Frankel as a board member or corporate officer. Unsurprisingly perhaps, he's been involved with at least 15 different companies over the years. An intriguing pattern also emerges. I'm finding other Frankels on some of the boards. When I begin searching them, I discover they're all related. My suspicions of the Frankel family are rising. All of their businesses seem to be tied to homebuilding, real estate, or lending.

Then I look for any records I can find on Thrift Bank Mortgage. Since I've found the names of the Frankel family's various companies, I search for links between them and Thrift Bank. Nothing emerges. After hours of fruitless searching, I give up and move on to a different subject.

I'm curious to know more about Dave Friedly, the Federal agent who left me the message I retrieved while in Miami. A search on his name yields a few entries for accomplishments in basketball during his college days. The best I can tell, he's in his early thirties. There's no indication where he currently lives, although he attended Georgetown. I search images and find one picture from his basketball days. The picture is at a distance so I can't make out facial features, but he's obviously tall and black. He has no social networking accounts or blog sites that I can find. I'm confident his lack of current web exposure is all by design. It seems Mr. Friedly likes to keep a low profile, which is pretty smart in his business.

My next search is for Don Opitz, the Thrift Bank executive who showed up at John's house the night before he died. This guy is stealth. I find nothing on him. I try various combinations of initials, last name spellings, you name it. Nothing. Knowing how rare it is for someone to have no digital footprint, I wonder if his non-existence in the digital world is the result of a well-orchestrated effort—or if Don Opitz is a fake name.

It's very late when the generator shuts off from a lack of fuel. There's no worry this time, as I still have enough for a couple of days. I wander out to the porch and light a candle. I had remembered to charge the iPod for the first time since arriving on Ballast, so I crank up some Eagles, take a couple of shots of leftover tequila, and soon find myself singing along to "Tequila Sunrise."

To my surprise, the rising sun finds me still on the porch. The iPod's laying on the couch beside me, tequila bottle lodged in my hand, and the foul taste of liquor lingers in my mouth. I head for the kitchen, but remember the generator needs attention. Still rubbing the crust from my eyes, I add fuel, start it up, and stumble into the kitchen to complete my morning ritual of black coffee and fruit.

After breakfast, I head over to the main house and do a quick walk through. Only the grounds are in need of attention, so I return with a trimmer and pruning saw. After an hour, the place is much improved. With frustration setting in due to my lack of progress on the files, I return to my quarters and continue reading the Grisham novel.

After a few hours of reading, the Grisham book still freshly on my mind, I walk out back and restart the generator. Since it's lunch time, I radio Gavin and check in. Afterward, I sit down at the computer with the remaining files from work. I begin searching all the different names on the paperwork—hoping something will surface. The larger commercial deals seem the most suspect, so I start with them. They're full of LLCs and smaller corporations simply followed by "Inc." It's easy to ascertain ownership on some, and not so easy on others. Unfortunately, to find the records you have to know which state the incorporation papers were filed in. It's a hit-or-miss process, but after a while I get the hang of it, and picking the right state becomes easier. It's time consuming but after making what feels like good progress, nothing stands out as odd or out of place. I print out the records and attach them to the files for future reference. So much for the brilliant idea I got from the Grisham novel. But I hold out hope that at some point these pieces will help bring this puzzle together.

It's time to eat again by the time I shut everything down. Still a little fuzzy from last night's solo tequila smack-down, I opt for a meal easy on the stomach. I light the grill and throw on a couple of burgers. Grill-heated green beans round out the menu, and in no time my belly's full and I'm sitting on the porch lost in thought.

I turn on the local news for a few minutes before heading off to bed. When they air an update on the story, sleep becomes impossible. They continue to report on Thrift Banks' fraudulent activity but make no effort to dig deeper. It's almost like they're only spewing out information the Feds are giving them. They mention me, and again show my picture, which pisses me off. Contemplating the complexity, it dawns on me that I need to attack. All of this "reporting"—if that's what you call it—is just regurgitating bad information that was spoon-fed to them. The most logical thing I can do is what I'm good at: stirring shit up.

Unable to sleep, I turn on the computer again and spend a few minutes searching for information on the reporter who'd just updated my story. She's easy to find. I print her email address, the station address and phone number, and a copy of her biography on the "About Me" page of the station website. I'm not sure what, if anything, I'll do with it. But I have an idea that might help turn the tables on this whole mess.

When the sun begins poking up in the east, I hear a boat moving in close to the island. I peek out the front window and see someone in a large cigarette boat tying off on the dock. I'm not expecting anyone. I move out the front door and quickly tuck in behind some palmettos. I hear someone yelling for me, but from the distance I don't recognize the voice. When the voice moves closer, it becomes obvious it's Rob. I get a quick look and see he's alone. When I step out, he yells at me to get moving. We need to get to Fort Myers quickly. The tone of his voice scares me.

I ask him how long we'll be gone. He shrugs, telling me he doesn't know—maybe a few days. I run into the shack and quickly gather my things. I'm careful to bring everything related to my case. Rob doesn't know it yet, but this little excursion might be just what I need to get things rolling in my favor. Within minutes we hurry down the dock walkway and hop onto the boat. The engine roars to life, and a few minutes later Ballast Key disappears behind us.

CHAPTER 16

September 17, 2008 7:00 a.m.

After about thirty minutes at high speed, Rob throttles back to idle as we move into a tiny canal. He begins telling me about a couple of guests Adriana had at Dante's last night. Apparently, two men were asking various bartenders if they'd seen me recently. When they made it to Adriana, she told them I'd been at the bar about a week ago and had left with some dark-haired woman from New York. She also told them I had departed on the Key West Express a few days later en route to Fort Myers. She described one of them as having beady-blue eyes.

I cringe, thinking these may be the same men Nikki saw the night John disappeared. Rob and I both think they're not the Feds. I ask Rob how we're getting to Fort Myers and why we're going when he suddenly turns toward a dock and parks the boat. His eyes meet mine intensely, and he says we need to take the heat off of Key West. He points at me and says I need to be seen—and that means confirmed sightings on cameras, making sure people remember me. It's a side of him I haven't seen before, and it's chilling. He adds that these guys were not playing around. They threatened Adriana with deportation and insinuated even worse if she was lying. He continues, saying that I might actually be apprehended. But if so, that's the way it has to be.

I can't believe what I'm hearing. I tell him, "No way! Why the hell should I go?" He steps close to me and screams in my face, "Gavin is old and can't take a lot of heat! Adriana is barely legal to be in the states and she lied about you getting on the boat!" Then he says he's busted his ass for me and now it's time for me to cover their asses. He continues, saying either I do this or I'm on my own. He clearly means it.

Things get quiet as I contemplate the circumstances. Knowing he's right doesn't make me want to oblige. The thing is, in the past I would have just left and figured it out on my own. But these people have given me a chance, maybe my only chance. They've taken me under their wings. It seems the least I can do is deflect attention away from Key West. The silence seems to last forever before I agree to go. If I get caught, at least I'll go down doing one thing right in my life.

Begrudgingly, I begin unloading my things as Rob tells me we're flying to Fort Myers. I look around and realize the dock is at a small island airstrip. Off in the distance I see several planes tied down. He tells me we've got access to a boat and a place to stay when we get to Fort Myers. With urgency in his eyes, he tells me not to worry. I'm uneasy, but Rob assures me he spent last night planning this trip and that I have a good chance of making it back to Ballast. His confidence doesn't help; I'm still nervous but strangely excited too.

Sugarloaf Shores Airpark is a small 2,700-foot strip about seventeen miles up U.S. 1 from Key West. Rob's old friend Don runs it. He's a mysterious looking guy with shoulder-length hair that camouflages a deep scar on the left side of his forehead. He simply hands Rob a set of keys and silently walks away. A quiet demeanor only adds to his mystique. I don't bother asking Rob what kind of business they used to do. It seems this area is full of people who've moved on from a past they don't care to re-visit, and they're more than willing to assist someone else in doing the same.

We quickly walk across the runway and load our things into a small Cessna 172. It's an early '60s model with very little in the way of updated equipment. Rob approaches with his bags. His last one strikes me as odd. It's a scraggly looking trash bag with holes in it. Hair protrudes out, and it's bulky to the point of being difficult to load in the plane. I ask what it is but he doesn't answer. When he hops into the co-pilot seat, I ask what he's doing. He tells me to fly the plane and he'll navigate. Exasperated, I tell him it's been a while since I've flown and he says that's OK; it's been a couple of years since he's navigated. I shake my head in frustration as he hands me a checklist. I begin going through the start-up procedure. When I request current aeronautical charts he hands me a two-year old sectional of South Florida. I ask him what the hell this is, and he says welcome to the bush leagues. He then pulls out a GPS and says our destination strip is 2,000-feet long. It's private, called Tranquility Bay and sits on Pine Island about twenty minutes by boat to the Key West Express' passenger terminal.

As I begin a pre-departure engine run-up, Rob instructs me to fly due north and stay below 300 feet. Once we reach Everglades Airpark, we'll climb to 3,500-feet and pick up radar service from Miami. He says he'll do the radio work, and we'll be using a false tail number for identification. Since we're landing at a private strip, no one will be the wiser.

He lightens up for just a minute, long enough to tell me he loves flying. But something is different about him today, and it makes me nervous.

Looking at the aircraft instrumentation, feeling the aircraft climb as I pull back on the wheel, and dialing in all of the control surfaces takes me back to my training. I find myself working the cockpit like an old professional, and for a few moments I forget about the trouble that lies ahead. It feels good.

Once I'm in level flight, I ask Rob what the hell's in the trash bag. He says I'll find out soon enough. His evasiveness just makes me more curious.

As we fly toward Everglades City, I gaze at the gorgeous view of the Gulf. Several fishing boats float along below. As I close in on them, Rob suggests I keep my distance. He doesn't want anyone to read the tail number on the plane. I do as he says, zigzagging my way across the open water. When we reach the tip of Florida, I fly directly over Everglades Airpark and begin climbing as Rob had instructed. He immediately radios Miami Center, requesting radar service to Pine Island Airport. I look at him with a "what the fuck" look as he just told me we were en route to Tranquility Bay. I'm unsure of what he's doing, although that's beginning to feel normal. When I look closer at the old chart, I notice Pine Island has five private airstrips within four miles of each other. It suddenly dawns on me that this trick would seriously confuse anyone trying to locate our plane. Driving to all five airports would be the only way to figure out which strip we actually landed at. Rob never ceases to amaze me. He's obviously been down this road before.

As we near Fort Myers' airspace, Rob requests a descent. The controller grants the request and immediately instructs us to turn west of the Fort Myers Airport. He then hands our radar service over to Fort Myers. I begin a gradual descent. He tells me to be no higher than 1,000 feet when I reach the beach. I fly as instructed and within a few minutes we're west of the beach headed north with Pine Island coming into view. As I pass over the tip of Sanibel Island, Rob radios Fort Myers, telling them he has Pine Island Airport in sight. He then has me descend to 400 feet and points out Tranquility Bay.

The strip is well hidden between two canals that lead directly into the Matlacha Pass. The canals are deep enough for boat access and I can see a dock at the east end of the property. Some sort of fishing boat sits atop a lift under the covered portion. The aerial view of this place is telling. It sits in a secluded, undeveloped portion of the island. Access by car is limited, providing the perfect hideaway. I can only imagine how much contraband has been pushed through this salty piece of land. It's obvious Rob has been here many times, but I ask no questions. He asks if I can handle a slam-dunk landing. I tell him, "You bush league guys are nuts, but I'll try."

The runway runs east-west so I maneuver the aircraft into perfect position for a landing to the east. Rob says not to sweat it. If I miss, we can stay low and go around for another try. I slow the plane as much as possible before killing the throttle and letting the plane sink into the unkempt shaggy, grass strip. When I cross the runway threshold, the plane floats along using precious runway. I begin to relax as the wheels touch down. Rob smarts off, saying he thought I'd miss it the first time. I exhale, mumbling at him to fuck off.

We taxi to a house at the east end of the strip. It's dilapidated, looking as though time passed it by. Several broken-down, rusty old cars sit adjacent to it, and a mangy farm dog meanders the property, discouraging nosy outsiders. When we exit the plane, Rob immediately grabs the taxi-tow-bar, and we begin pushing the aircraft to a spot beneath the canopy of a large tree, effectively camouflaging it. After we cover all sides with netting, the aircraft nearly disappears.

Rob points out an old metal building sitting about fifty yards from the house. He says there's a bunk-room in it and we'll be sleeping there if we make it back this evening. Otherwise, we'll sleep in the cabin of the boat we're taking to the marina.

We carry our things to the building and enter the bunk-room. A musty smell and concrete floors greet us, and it feels like an old youth hostel. It has bunk beds made of scrap wood, an old console TV with a digital converter box attached to it, and a bathroom that reminds me of something I'd see in a gas station on I-95. It's obvious the owner set this up so wayward pilots and boaters could stay here without needing access to the main house. I set my first bag down and hurriedly return to the plane for more. Once everything is unloaded, Rob reaches into the rear cabin storage and pulls out magnetic numbers and long pieces of magnetic striping. Within five minutes, our plane has a new tail number and a color change. I hardly recognize it. Rob cracks his first smile of the day, brags on his handy work, and tells me you never know when a curious sheriff's deputy might happen by.

After all of our bags are placed in the bunk-room, we sit down for a few minutes. We call Gavin on the cell phones he had acquired for this trip and let him know we're on the ground. He says all is well in Key West. We agree to check back with him later this evening.

At this point, I tell Rob I want to call Brett's attorney in Trenton. I have a copy of my computer files on one of the external hard drives, and I want him to have it. Since we're away from Key West, there's no better time to make the call and mail the hard drive. Rob agrees. I dial Pete Hoyt, attorney at law. After giving his secretary my name, he immediately picks up the phone. I ask him if he's making any progress on Brett's case and he firmly states he can't discuss it. I tell him that's fine, but he'd better figure out who his allies are and that I'm one of them. I tell him about my computer files and that I want him to have them. There's a long pause when finally he asks why. I explain that if Brett can find something that helps him, it will probably help me as well. I ask him where he wants me to send an overnight package. He rattles off the address. I tell him to expect it tomorrow. He says thanks, and as I hear him offering his services to me, I hang up.

Rob and I sit, brainstorming about today's upcoming events. He knows the marina area well and mentions a bar where he wants me to spend time. He has picked out a rendezvous point he wants to use if we get split up. Seeming more like his old self, he says if things go well for me, I'll want to use the rendezvous point even if I don't need it. Puzzled, I ask what the hell he's talking about. He just smiles.

I suddenly feel the need to thank him again for all he, Gavin, and even Adriana have done. I explain how under normal circumstances I couldn't imagine risking my ass like this. But with all that's happened, I feel a strong sense of loyalty to all of them. I can't imagine anyone risking everything to help me.

Rob sits, quietly listening to me, and finally says he's not sure he would have helped to this extent if not for John showing up dead in Miami. He continues, saying the only thing he knows for sure is that I'm not a murderer. And if someone is trying to frame me for that, they're probably trying to pin even more dirty laundry on me. I tell him that I'm tired and that I am beginning to understand his feelings about money. At this moment I don't even care about my frozen bank accounts. Then I shrug, asking him if he saw the news the other day. The stock market hit a fresh ten-year low, which means I probably don't have much money left anyway. We both utter a mournful chuckle.

I decide it's time to discuss my idea from last night with Rob. I begin by pointing out that somebody's funneling bad information to the press, and, as he's aware, it's putting a lot of heat on me. I pose a couple of "what if" questions to him about providing information to that local TV reporter in Miami who's been reporting on the story. Her name is Elena Maria and she's with WHEV TV, the local Fox affiliate. He remarks that if she figures out where I am, we're all screwed. He's right, but I ignore his comment and continue explaining the different ways media coverage could pressure those trying to pin this mess on me. It takes a while, but after some convincing, Rob warms to the idea. It seems I can still close a deal. He finally decides that contacting her probably won't make the situation any worse. Since we need to discuss a game plan with Gavin anyway, we agree to deal with it later.

Rob then opens his bag, handing me a razor and hair clippers. He says sorry about the growth but I won't need a disguise today. I just shake my head and start trimming. It feels good to clean up. Rob warns me about trying to use the ATM card. Since I used it in Miami and then abruptly left, using it again will make it obvious I want to be tracked. I agree and tell him not to worry. I wonder aloud if I should just destroy all of my credit cards. He advises against that, saying some day life might be normal again.

It's barely 10 a.m. After the boat ride, plane ride and settling into the outbuilding, I'm so amped up I can't sit still. Rob feels the same, so he says to give him about thirty minutes and he'll be ready to hit the town. He grabs the bulky trash bag and disappears into the bathroom. A short while later he opens the door. I nearly bust a gut laughing. His hair is jet black; he has a mustache, a scar, and a smashed-in looking nose. The transformation is amazing. He starts laughing, telling me it's been many years since he had this look. He sits down and tells me he'll be using his alias "Ty." He continues, telling me he has identification supporting him as Ty Cogdale. Then he pulls out a tiny camera he'll have placed in his hat, explaining that if we run into someone—we'll want pictures. I make a quick trip into the bathroom and ready myself for the day. Afterward, "Ty" and I depart the bunkroom and head down to the boat.

CHAPTER 17

September 17, 2008 11:30 a.m.

We reach the dock quickly and find the boat in pristine condition. Its twin 175-horsepower Honda engines look as though they've never been used. The boat's fiberglass finish is spotless and the chrome hand railings shine like they just came out of the factory. The small cuddy cabin is clean but dated. The cushions are obvious '80s holdovers, but spotless nonetheless.

After giving the boat a thorough inspection, we stow our overnight bags in the cabin. I'm concerned about the hard-drive Rob's mailing, so I take special precautions to keep it dry. Once the boat's lowered in the water, both engines start easily. We begin backing out when Rob asks if I have any boating experience. I nod my head yes, but explain it's with smaller lake-bound boats. He explains the basics of twin-engine operation. It looks easy, especially with this boat.

As we begin idling down the Matlacha Pass toward Fort Myers, we discuss how these guys might have known to look for me at Dante's. We suspect the northeastern girl with whom I had enjoyed a short-lived friendship called the authorities after seeing my picture on the news. It makes me sick, but Rob agrees that since the guys looking for me fit the same description as those who were with John when he disappeared, it's likely a dirty Fed is involved.

We talk about the reporter option. He begins to understand how I hope to harness some investigative resources by using her to find information for us. In his usual, off-the-cuff style, he jokes that I probably just want to fuck her. He has a knack at delivering his message in a way that makes you laugh, even in the worst of times. But I have to agree, she is hot.

We idle toward the channel talking about today's plans. We both understand it's very risky. I make it clear to Rob that if anyone apprehends me, he's to make sure the reporter gets the case files I left at Tranquility Bay. He agrees. I tell him her contact information is taped to the inside pocket of the black Samsonite suitcase. He says to relax and that it'll be a walk in the park, almost like he believes it.

Once in the channel, the engines roar to life and in fifteen minutes we're making our way under the Sanibel Causeway, turning east with the San Carlos Bridge coming into view. Rob throttles back and eases the boat toward the end of a finger-like canal to a little pub called the Surf Club. We tie off on the canal wall, careful not to obstruct anyone's boat slip access. Rob shuffles around for a few minutes, grabbing the hard-drive and one of his overnight bags. He departs, telling me to wait in the cabin while he's gone.

Nearly an hour passes before he returns. I'm drenched with sweat and nearly passed out from the heat when Rob sticks his head into the cabin and starts laughing at me. He calls me a dumb ass as he flips a switch for the AC. He sits down to catch his breath and informs me the package is headed to Trenton.

He hands me a map and a key. The key's to a place called The Crackajack Motel, which sits a half-mile south of the Surf Club on Estero Boulevard. The place is a dump but it's perfect. It's located on the less populated south end of the beach. It's cheap, and the guy running it doesn't check ID, which means "Ty" didn't have to risk using his alias. I'm to wait there if we get split up for any reason.

With our first task complete, Rob starts the boat and we idle out of the canal toward the main channel. Once there, we turn east and I immediately see the Key West Express at its dock. Rob explains that we're going to a place called Salty Sam's Marina. It sits next door to the Key West Express terminal, and the place is always packed when a ship comes in.

Before parking the boat, Rob passes the marina and reaches into the cabin, pulling out some stick-on numbers. Within a few minutes our boat has a new registration number. Once again Rob smiles, and I shake my head as I experience a feeling of growing respect for my very capable new friend.

We float up to the end of dock-D, and Rob ties off the boat. He says it's showtime and points toward The Parrot Key Restaurant. It's time for me to make some friends, something I do easily, but apprehension is written all over my face. He again tells me not to sweat it, that he'll be hanging back—watching and waiting. He wants me to stay most of the day, but when the bar begins to thin out, he instructs me to meander toward the boat so we can move somewhere that allows overnight docking. If no one's trailing, he'll catch up. If there's a tail, I'll have to get creative and make my way to the Crackajack. I manage a smile and say, "OK, Ty," shrug, and begin walking into a public place for the first time since my picture was broadcast all over the airwaves.

My heart's pounding out of my chest as I take a seat at the back corner of the bar. The seat gives me an unobstructed view of the entire establishment. From here, no one can get behind me. It's a good thing I've seen a few cowboy movies. Also, I have a gorgeous view of the port, the boats parked at the marina, and the hotels across the Intracoastal at Fort Myers Beach. It feels strange to be out in public. I keep wondering if everyone's looking at me. It's then I realize that controlling paranoia is going to be crucial.

I order a beer from a sexy middle-aged bartender. She brings the beer, and we start chatting. Her name's Daphne and she has an accent I can't quite place. It turns out she's one of those people who travels around the world working in the tourism industry. She might be in the Bahamas for the winter and then off to Australia for their ski season in the spring. She raves about it, telling me I should try it. Under the circumstances, I can't help but agree. After a little more bar talk, I learn that Italy's home.

The bar fills up as the Key West Express disembarks her passengers, quite a few of them already drunk from the four-hour ride. Most are jovial but hungry. I keep an eye out for anyone suspicious, especially someone with light-colored hair and beady blue eyes. The volume rises in the bar as people begin talking over each other. Thankfully no one tries to strike up a conversation with me. I simply watch, listen, and wait.

Across the room, I catch my first glimpse of "Ty." He's got a beer and he's blending in as one of the tourists scurrying around the Parrot Key Grill. He sits, talking to drunken patrons while keeping an eye on what's going on in the bar. As I watch, I feel myself relax a little, knowing he's there.

Sitting at the bar, my mind begins to drift. I still can't rationalize why these people from Key West have rallied to my defense. It's baffling. All my years in the corporate world taught me to be wary of those who are "helping" you. They always want something in return. But that doesn't seem to fit with these Key West people. They seem to operate under a different set of rules. They've asked me for nothing, except for this. Under the circumstances, a reasonable request. I've never seen money change hands, and it's never been discussed. I have no idea how much they're spending to keep me hidden, but the longer this takes, the more it'll cost.

A couple of hours pass and The Parrot begins to clear out. "Ty" nonchalantly motions toward the boat, so I wave Daphne over for the check. She obliges and comments that I had only three beers all day. She hadn't figured out my little trick and I was glad. It's amazing how easy it is to fill your beer bottle with water. No one ever knows the difference. As I pay the tab, I ask where I might find a good karaoke bar. She smiles, telling me that she and her friends are heading to a place called Nemo's later this evening, and she'd love for me to join them. I gladly accept, and ask what time they plan to arrive. With a friendly smile she says, "Sunset." If I weren't in so much trouble, I think I know where I'd be spending the night, or at least, with whom.

I wander around the dock for a few minutes, casually making sure I'm visible on the security cameras. "Ty" tactically chose slot No. 6, due to its distance from The Parrot and its proximity to the cameras. Since they're nearly useless to the end slips, no one can see which boat we're actually using. Taking extra precautions when boarding, I duck behind a boat-lift, slide onto our vessel and down into the cuddy cabin. This time I flip the switch for the AC. Approximately fifteen minutes later, "Ty" sneaks back onto the boat, unties us, and fires the engines. We idle across the main channel back to the canal where the Surf Club sits.

This time we dock at one of the private slips owned by the Silver Sands Motel. I hole up in the cabin while "Ty" makes arrangements for the boat to stay in the slip overnight. He returns with a lady named Andrea, and the two of them place a permit on the boat giving us access until tomorrow.

It's nearly six o'clock by the time we're ready to leave the boat. Since we don't want to be seen together, Rob decides to walk down Estero Boulevard and pick up some junk food at a local Seven-Eleven. When he returns, he hands me a hot dog, chips and a Diet Coke. I grumble thanks for considering my health. Then he hands me another cell phone, saying we'll use it to call the reporter tomorrow.

After our delectable dinner, Rob decides it's time to call Gavin. He wants me to tell him about the reporter idea. Gavin says very little until I'm finished. After a long pause, he says under the circumstances it's probably a smart idea. He continues, saying my situation is far more complex than either his or Rob's were, and a different approach is probably warranted.

He suggests calling her first, followed by a brief email. If she's willing to get involved, we can then overnight enough information to get her started. If things go well from there, and if it's necessary, maybe we'll arrange a meeting.

He says this might work without ever seeing her face-to-face—which might be preferable.

We agree that sending her an email and calling from Fort Myers is smart. If anyone's tracking my movements, they'll be looking for me here instead of Key West. With that settled, Rob and I agree to track down Elena tomorrow.

For now, it's off to Nemo's for beer, Karaoke, and a certain sexy bartender named Daphne.

CHAPTER 18

September 17, 2008 6:45 p.m.

Once again, I step off the boat and into the unknown. I walk past the entrance to the Surf Club and quickly cross Estero Boulevard en route to Nemo's. I scurry down a wooden walkway leading to an open-air, beach-level bar. The view is jaw-dropping. The entire backside opens onto the sugar sands of Fort Myers Beach. Flip-flops and T-shirts are standard attire. Perfect for me. I love the place and want to relax, but I'm too stressed. I walk the entire bar, familiarizing myself with all the exits. I find two good options for a quick departure, and one is only steps away. Surely a few beers will calm me.

I find a seat at the bar giving me a good view of anyone walking in. An older, heavy-set blonde is hooking up the Karaoke machine, and a few groups of happy-hour holdovers are hammering down pitchers of cheap beer. I order a draft and wait for Daphne and her crew to arrive. My heart's thumping out of my chest again so I slam the first draft and immediately order another. Fortunately, "Ty" enters and takes a seat across the bar. At least I have backup.

Right on schedule, Daphne and her posse arrive just as the sun is setting on the Gulf. They're fired up and ready to party. Her friends are two nice-looking blondes, one of them with boyfriend in tow. The crew orders shots and chant, " It's on!" Normally I'd be all over this, but not tonight. Daphne chats me up and hands me a shot of Jägermeister. I down the shot and feel its sweet, oily burn instantly calm me. The conversation immediately picks up and before long the alcohol begins to beautify Daphne. Alcohol, hormones, or both, and my mind shifts from trouble to pleasure.

It doesn't take long for the Karaoke DJ to start asking for volunteers. We ignore her, knowing it'll take more liquid courage to start singing. The volume slowly rises to near deafening as the bar fills up. The Karaoke list is five deep by the time Daphne signs me up. She gets a little touchy, gently coaxing me to sing. She says I'll be her star. She has no idea. For the next few minutes, I completely forget my troubles, and it feels great.

When my name comes up to sing, I take the stage and see "Ty" clapping. I smirk at him when the intro for Toby Keith's "I Love This Bar" starts playing. I dive into the first verse, and by the time I make it to the chorus, the crowd joins in. By the third verse the place is raucous. I'm not sure if it's my singing, the booze, or just a good song, but it's fun. When I'm done, Daphne grabs me, cups my face in her hands and hits me with a nice, wet kiss. It feels fantastic.

Just as Daphne orders another round of drinks, I see "Ty" move toward two men. It's not his usual type of movement. It seems hurried so I watch carefully. He pulls out a tourist type digital camera and casually snaps a few pictures. This move perplexes me, as I know he has a small camera hidden in his ball cap. A moment later, our drinks arrive and Daphne pulls me towards the beach, suggesting we go for a walk. I gladly oblige but look back, checking on "Ty." Nothing seems out of the ordinary.

We walk a few steps south and stumble across a beach party at a hotel called the Lani Kai. Fire-breathers, torch jugglers, and a band are performing on a stage that faces the beach. Picnic tables and a bonfire round out the amenities. At least a couple hundred people are dancing and drinking. Daphne tells me The Lani Kai puts this party on four nights a week during the high season, and it's the biggest draw around. We find an empty table and sit. It's dark and hard to see but I catch a faint glimpse of "Ty" shadowing me.

The light from the fire pit, the juggling torches, and the stage give off a gaseous glow to the surrounding beach area. It's disconcerting, as I can't make out facial features. As I sit on the picnic table, Daphne with her arms around me, kissing my cheek, I catch a glimpse of two guys who seem out of place. They're moving through the crowd, looking at people, and then moving on. "Ty" moves toward them but they reach me first. Suddenly, one tries to grab me, alarming Daphne. A scuffle ensues, drawing the attention of the party's bouncers. I push one of the men into the other and take off at full speed. Adrenaline pulsates through me, but the alcohol makes me weak in the knees. I hear people yelling as I frantically run past them. After a few minutes, I look back and see a shadow pacing behind. If it were "Ty," he'd yell for me—so I keep running.

I reach The Neptune on the south end of the beach. The motel has a pool and a bunch of barbecue grills overlooking the beach. I break left, sprinting into the parking lot. Once I see the exit to Estero Boulevard, I cross the street, carefully looking for the Crackajack. I can still hear people yelling at my pursuer, informing him of my direction. What are these people thinking?

The Crackajack's sign leaves a lot to be desired. Most of the light bulbs are burned out. When I get close, I realize I'm fucked. The three drunks out front see me as plain as day. I continue past the place and begin looking for a corner to duck in and hide. I run to the end of Delmar Avenue. There's no way out. Out of desperation, I jump a fence, run through someone's back yard, and then jump another fence. The next thing I know I'm running back towards Estero. Dogs are barking, telling me someone is still in pursuit. I'm sweating profusely and nearly out of breath when I jump yet another fence, and take refuge in a back-yard with no dogs. Two kayaks and a canoe are leaning against a storage shed so I quickly crawl in behind them. My legs are shaking and I'm gasping for air as I lay on the bare ground, flat on my back. Dogs continue barking, but not near me. I just hope no one is home.

Nearly an hour later, I've cooled off and caught my breath. The trouble is, I'm still too scared to call "Ty." Fear of being seen again, or making any noise, has me paralyzed. I know I'll have to move along at some point. But when?

After another hour, I pull myself out from under the canoe and peek around. No lights are on and no sound of barking dogs. I'm itchy and miserable from the plethora of mosquito bites I've endured. I begin moving again. This time, I jump the fence to the next street and quietly move towards Estero Boulevard. Somewhere in the back of my mind, I've decided to attempt a reunion with "Ty" at our boat.

I stumble across Bayview Street, which parallels Estero. Finally I make progress without having to jump fences. I follow Bayview, happy to see no streetlights. But once I reach the end of Bayview, it's evident I'll be using my track and field skills again. I carefully select another house, jump the fence and end up near a post office. At this point, I tuck in behind a dumpster and call

"Ty." He suspects he's being tailed and doesn't know how long it'll take him to reach the boat. He's relieved to hear I'm still on the loose but tells me under no circumstances am I to go to the boat. He wants me to find a safe place and hide. Exasperated, I pull out the little tourist map he gave me earlier. After perusing it for a few minutes, one place comes to mind, and it's covered.

I stay put for another hour, hoping my pursuers have given up for the night. Finally, I begin moving again. Jumping fences is getting old, but again I find it necessary in order to stay off of Estero Boulevard. Somehow, I make my way to Crescent Street and am able to walk toward the San Carlos Bridge without the worry of being seen. Since most of the tourist traffic is bottlenecked on Estero, the side streets remain relatively quiet, especially in the wee hours of the morning.

I reach the bridge and look up, finding it just as I remembered from yesterday. I follow an incline up to the point where the road meets the suspended portion, making a perfect place to hole up for the night. Homeless people figured out the value of bridges a long time ago. Reflecting on my plight, I'm humbled by the tapestry of life. It's amazing how circumstances can lead you to a place you never imagined possible. But I feel lucky. The bridge is vacant tonight.

Chapter 19

September 18, 2008 1:30 a.m.

My nerves are shot and I feel exhaustion descending upon me. But there's no way I can let myself fall into a deep sleep. I set the phone next to my ear and lay back against the concrete. My mind is racing. Who are these guys? Are they Feds? Wouldn't the Feds have back-up law enforcement? Since I've yet to see any local police searching the area, I can only think that these guys are protecting Thrift Bank interests. Either way, I'm better off getting apprehended by law enforcement. I just hope I've made enough of a scene to get out of Fort Myers for good. I guess Rob will be the judge of that.

It's nearly daybreak when the phone vibrates. It's Rob and he's finally made it back to the boat. He asks my location. When I tell him, he laughs and asks how I slept. He quickly realizes I'm in no mood for humor, but he's pleased that I'm close by. He instructs me to move toward the water when I see him pull out of the canal. Once he's close, he wants me to swim to the boat.

Until now, running shoes have been a blessing. However, as I walk deeper into the water, swimming becomes difficult. I struggle but manage to make it just outside of the first bridge piling when Rob tosses out a short rope. He walks to the shore side of the boat and begins nonchalantly fishing. I use all of my remaining energy to get over the railing, finally collapsing onto the fiberglass floor of the boat. Rob ignores me, continuing to fish while I crawl into the cabin. He allows the outgoing tide to carry the boat past the bridge and then casually fires the engines. We idle into the channel, and he pushes the throttles forward. A few minutes later, we're motoring toward the safe haven of Tranquility Bay.

I stay in the cabin below while we thunder up the Matlacha Pass. When Rob throttles the engines back, I peek out. He pulls the boat onto the lift and says the coast is clear. We begin unloading our things and move toward the bunk-house. Once there, complete exhaustion sets in. We both collapse, neither of us in the mood to talk.

The rustic, dirty shower feels like heaven. Hot water, soap, and a washcloth have never felt better. After showering, I sit down and turn on the antiquated TV. The local morning newscast is playing so I watch intently. Nothing is mentioned about my chase. Unsure of what to make of last night's activity, I stagger to the bunks, crawl into a dusty bed, and quickly drift off to sleep.

It's early afternoon when I awake. After yesterday, six hours of sleep is not nearly enough, but sufficient for a normal thought process. I stumble around, looking for something to drink. The refrigerator is stocked with water, juices, and power bars. I dive in. Even a power bar tastes great in my famished state. Rob begins moving after hearing the commotion. He sits up, shakes his head and says he thought Daphne was cute. Dejected, I moan about wanting her last night. He chuckles, telling me he has no doubt she wanted me, too.

The conversation turns to what happened after I high-tailed it away from the Lani Kai. Rob made sure to trip the second of my pursuers. He says the bouncer escorted that guy off the property. The one chasing me, according to Rob, had light-colored hair. He has pictures, but doesn't know how good they are.

I ask about the guys at Nemo's. He's unsure, but suspects they might be working together. He has pictures of them—good quality he believes.

Still trying to wake up, I turn on the computer. I want a closer look at Rob's pictures. I also want to start writing an email to Elena introducing myself and providing information she'll need. Rob watches what I'm doing and reminds me Gavin said to call her first. He's right. What if she has no interest in this? In reality, all TV reporters do is show up at the scene of a newsworthy event and give a short oratory about what happened. They rarely, if ever, investigate anything. Alas, the news-bunny term. It's possible she'll simply turn over my information to authorities and I'll still be fucked. But that's a risk I'm willing to take.

With apprehension, I dig out the phone Rob purchased yesterday and prepare to call her. He immediately stops me, warning that if she rolls over on me, authorities will be able to pinpoint which cell towers the call bounced off of. That will give them a good idea of how we slipped in and out of Fort Myers. He suggests we take the boat downtown and make the call from a dock. And he says we should be ready to move quickly after the call is made.

For now, I return to writing the email—just in case Elena agrees to take this on. I give Rob another hard drive, copies of the Internet searches, and the names and phone numbers of those who left me voice mails when all of this started. He begins packaging them for overnight delivery.

Before I've finished the email, Rob pulls out the two cameras he used last night. The hat-cam did pretty well. It took three clear pictures of the guys at Nemo's, and the hand-held digital took a couple of clear side shots. The two guys at Lanai Kai are lucky. Only two usable pictures emerge and they're poor quality. We hope Adriana will recognize someone from these pictures. I go ahead and attach all of them to Elena's pending email.

The email details my suspicions of the Frankel family, my connections to Brett Bowers in Trenton, and my conversation with Nikki Marris, John's wife. I also describe all of the interest in the files I took from the office. While I don't plan to send those files along in the package, I let her know I have them. It's a little deceptive since some of the files are gone, but explaining what happened to them feels like telling your teacher the dog ate your homework. What I'm sending should be enough to get her started. I just hope this "reporter" has enough journalist in her to make something happen.

With everything ready, we leave the house en route to the docks in downtown Fort Myers. Our route takes us south toward Sanibel Island, but this time we turn west at the Caloosahatchee River. Shortly after turning upriver, we spot a crab shack called Pinchers under the Caloosahatchee Bridge. Rob idles toward their docks and ties off at the far end. His look is still significantly altered. He lost his crumpled nose while showering this morning. But the jet-black hair and a fake mustache remain. He puts on sunglasses and a ball cap when the restaurant deck hand approaches. I disappear into the cabin while he makes short-term parking arrangements. Once the deck hand is gone, Rob pokes his head into the cabin and says he's going into the restaurant for a bite. He cuts up, snarkily telling me to enjoy my call to the news-bunny. I snidely flip him the bird.

I dial the main number for WHEV-TV and a receptionist, an older woman I think, answers the call. Without hesitation I ask for Elena Maria. The receptionist asks who's calling. When I tell her it's Pete Johnson, she asks if Elena is expecting my call. I tell her no but I'm quite confident she'd enjoy hearing from me. While I know that's an overstatement, it exudes enough confidence for the receptionist to request that I hold for a minute. When she returns, she says Elena will have to call me back and that she'll put me through to voice mail. Disgusted, I simply tell Elena who I am and that I need to speak with her ASAP. I leave the disposable cell number and explain that I can't wait long. Afterwards, I wait for Rob and hope for a return call.

Rob arrives first so I tell him about the message. He grumbles and complains that we can't wait long. After a short debate, we decide it wouldn't hurt for me to be seen in Fort Myers one more time. There's a Best Western within walking distance and it has free WiFi access. Better, there are security cameras everywhere. Even though I haven't spoken with Elena, we decide to go ahead with the email. My reasoning is that if she decides against the story and forwards the information to authorities, what would it hurt?

I step off the boat and walk with determination toward the Best Western. Strangely, I have little fear this time. I'm all business. The two-block walk only takes a few minutes.

I walk into the lobby, careful to look as though I belong, and immediately sit down in clear view of the cameras. After the computer boots up, I begin setting up another dummy email account. I use Hotmail and in less than five minutes, the email is on its way to Elena.

As I'm shutting the computer down, the phone rings.

CHAPTER 20

September 18, 2008 4:00 p.m.

My palms sweat when I see the caller ID. It's the WHEV switchboard number, which causes my stomach to knot up. I quickly slip the computer into its carrying case and throw it over my shoulder. While walking out the lobby door, I answer the call. An inquisitive Elena Maria says hello and without wasting any time, asks why I called.

I ignore her question and ask if she's recording the conversation. Without missing a beat, she answers yes. Since she'd need a minute to set up a recorder, I suspect that's why my original call was sent to voice mail. But it doesn't bother me, and I let her know that.

I explain that I saw her segment on the news a couple of nights ago and that the information she's reporting is false. I ask why no one in the media is actually investigating Thrift Bank Mortgage, its owners, and board members. The coverage, I continue, is simply regurgitating information I'm sure the Feds are releasing. I then ask if she has any desire to find the truth. Silence permeates the moment before she asks why she should talk to someone wanted for murder.

It's a brutal question, but one I expected. I answer by asking a question. Why, if I was in Miami to murder my ex-boss, would I turn on my cell phone, allowing me to be tracked, use my ATM card at the bank, and then kill him? It makes no sense. And why would I want to murder him anyway? I had already quit my job and left Jacksonville. I tell her of my suspicion that someone involved in the fraud case knew I was in Miami. They then dumped John there, making it appear as if I did it. It's a salacious story; one they knew the media would eat up, making movement nearly impossible for me.

She cuts in at this point, asking why someone would want John dead in the first place? I tell her I'm unsure, but suspect he knew more about Thrift Bank business affairs than someone was comfortable with. When they realized the files were missing, and found out I was in Miami, they killed John, simultaneously making me a suspect. Maybe they think heat on me will make it easier to retrieve the missing files, or that a murder rap discredits me as a witness. Either way, it's a win for them.

She smarts off, saying it sounds weak and convenient for me to come up with a story like this. I agree, but tell her the only reason I was in Miami that night was to make sure the Feds were looking for me in the wrong place. When I tell her I was in Miami for less than two hours and left by midnight she asks where I was. I give her the locations of the bank, the dock, and even the destination of the boat Rob tossed the Blackberry in. I also remind her that the story broke on the national news around 10:00 a.m. the next day, giving John's murderers all night to kill him and dump his body. They could have been anywhere in Florida and had time to get to Miami. It's not much for her to go on, but it's a start. I implore her to verify the details. I also suggest she inquire with Miami authorities and get as much information from them as she can. Sarcastically, she reminds me that she's the reporter here. I chuckle, thinking she may have the fire in her belly I was hoping for.

She asks why I went into hiding when the story originally broke. I explain how I was enjoying some down-time at a bar when the story came on Fox News. They mentioned how wiretaps picked up talk of some missing files in the Jacksonville office. That talk triggered raids all across the country. I tell her it was me who took the files and she asks why. I tell her I took them out of spite because I was pissed off, and that I have no idea what's so incriminating in them. She then asks why I didn't just turn them over. I explain that I hadn't knowingly defrauded anyone during my years with Thrift Bank and I wasn't going down without a fight. I was determined not to be a fall guy for a criminal enterprise I was unaware existed. The files at least give me a bargaining chip. She questions me, saying she has a hard time believing I was oblivious to the fraud. We continue discussing Thrift Bank, and slowly she begins to understand that even as a senior underwriter, I wouldn't be privy to the kind of information that would warrant a nationwide raid.

As I walk toward the dock the traffic makes it difficult to hear. I'm also struggling with how to explain what's happened, so I ask if she's near a computer. She is, and I immediately suggest she check her email. She fumbles around briefly, finally seeing an odd email with a tag line of "PJ." I tell her it contains information about my case.

I begin explaining my searches on Thrift Bank and its executives. When I tell her about the Senator Frankel connection, she stops me, saying that's a stretch. "Is it?" I ask. I reiterate that enough information exists to warrant a look. I then ask if she knows how many businesses Bernie Frankel's family has related to mortgages, building, or real estate. She says she doesn't know, so I suggest she look with an open mind.

She asks why I don't just turn myself in, get representation, and sort this whole thing out. It's a fair question, but I tell her, "No way! Someone is trying to put me away for a long time by making it look like I killed my ex-boss." Further, I tell her it's likely that someone high in the food chain is trying to kill me. I continue, telling her the pictures attached to the email are people who were chasing me last night in Fort Myers Beach. And the funny thing is—the news media hasn't even reported it and there were no law enforcement officers involved.

She asks if I'm staying in Fort Myers. I tell her I'm moving around a lot. But for now, yes, I'll be here. It's a lie, but I can't let her know where I'm staying. It's just too risky for everyone involved.

There's no way I can answer all of her questions in one phone call. I tell her about the package I plan to send, explaining that it consists of a backup hard drive of my work computer, copies of my Internet searches, and the names and numbers of the people who seem to be looking for me. She says she'd like to see it. Relieved, I tell her to expect it tomorrow.

We've been talking nearly twenty minutes. She only commits to looking over the information. She asks if I'm sending along the missing files from the office. When I tell her no, she asks why. I reply that I don't trust her enough to give up my trump card just yet. But maybe I can figure out a way for her to peruse them at some point. That pisses her off, which pleases me. She needs to understand that trust is a two-way street.

She asks how to contact me and I tell her she'll have to wait until I call. I promise to communicate regularly and then request her cell phone number. She gives it to me, and I tell her about my satellite phone but explain the three-minute rule. I also tell her she can answer my emails to the address they're sent from one time. After that she'll get the next email from a different address. It will always have the initials "PJ" somewhere in the subject line. Last, she asks when we'll meet. I tell her that I honestly don't know.

I'm sitting in the boat cabin by the time Elena and I finish our conversation. Rob is at the captain's seat finishing his lunch. I stick my head out and tell him Elena is a "go" and he can mail the package. He finishes his last couple of bites and points to a small brown paper sack. It's a sandwich, fries, and coleslaw. All this talk has given me an appetite. I dive in.

Rob disappears for nearly twenty minutes. He returns and says the package is headed to Miami. Like a man on a mission, he grabs his phone, dials Gavin and checks in. Gavin seems a little pissed because he didn't hear from us earlier, but is pleased things have gone OK. As expected, all is well in Key West. He wants to know when we'll be back. Rob suggests we fly back first thing in the morning. I agree. Flying at night under bush league rules does not appeal to me.

Before starting the boat, I ask if a call to my buddy Arthur in Arizona would be too risky. Rob doesn't think so. In fact, if someone is listening in on his phone, it will further confirm our location. I pull out his number and call. As usual, voice mail. I leave a message explaining a few things, specifically, not to believe the murder story. I thank him for checking on me and that I'll be in touch when I get this mess worked out. Rob smiles, pats me on the shoulder and starts the boat. Within a few minutes, we're motoring up the Matlacha Pass towards Tranquility Bay.

CHAPTER 21

September 18, 2008 7:30 p.m.

It's late in the day by the time we return to Tranquility Bay. We park the boat, properly stow the excess boating equipment, and methodically snap on the custom canvas cover. Just before departing the dock, Rob reaches back and removes the stick-on registration numbers. I feel good knowing that the next time I leave here I'll be on a plane.

Walking towards the bunkhouse, the conversation turns to Elena. Rob's curious about our chat and whether I think she can be trusted. While my gut says she won't sell me out, I tell him I'm going to be careful until we see what she does.

Thankfully, it's a slow-paced, quiet evening. Rob and I play cards and pass the time. We returned too late for the network news, so a couple of re-run sit-coms provide background noise. After a while, the discussion turns to Gavin. Rob confides in me that Gavin wants to retire from the daily grind of the motel. His problem is finding people he can trust to run it and keep him flush with enough cash to relax. He also wants to buy a fishing boat, one big enough to sleep in. Boating the East Coast has always been his dream, but finding the time has been impossible. Rob plans to help him and hopes the old man's health holds out.

Fatigue from last night's adventure catches up with me so I head for the bunk room early. Rob's not far behind, as tomorrow looks to be another busy day. I lay in bed, slowly drifting off, wondering what the next few weeks and months are going to bring. The past few weeks seem almost unreal to me. But I feel better, now that I'm doing something.

It seems as though I just laid down when Rob wakes me, kicking the foot of my bed. He's bouncing off the walls, yet it's still dark outside. When I look at the clock, I grumble, as it's barely 6 a.m. He wants out of here at sunrise, so I get up and stumble around for a minute, finally becoming coherent.

After a few minutes of flight planning, we walk toward the plane and begin loading our things. We remove the magnetic striping and numbers, and then untie the camouflage netting. After a thorough pre-flight inspection, we tow the plane out from under the tree.

The winds are light out of the west, which saves us the trouble of taxiing to the opposite end of the strip. The air is thick with humidity and the salty, sulfur aroma reminds me just how close we are to the water. When the sun begins peeking above the eastern sky, it becomes evident how clear the skies really are. Smooth air and sunny skies are always welcome in a small aircraft. Couple that with returning to the safe-haven of Ballast Key, and I couldn't be happier about this day.

We do a quick final walk-through of the bunkhouse and lock the place up. We take our seats in the plane, again me flying and Rob handling the radio and navigation. The engine fires, and I go through all the standard engine tests. Everything is in order. I taxi the aircraft into position and push the throttles to full power. Within seconds, we're off the ground and flying over Pine Island Airport at one hundred feet. I continue the climb and turn south. Once I reach five hundred feet, Rob contacts Fort Myers Approach, uses another fake tail number, and picks up radar service to Everglades City. I roll my eyes, knowing he has some sort of trick up his sleeve. I climb to 3,500 feet and level off for the short flight.

I begin descending about ten miles north of Everglades City. Rob has me line up for landing on Runway 15 and then cancels radar service. Before we land, he tells me to break off, follow the coast south, and stay at two hundred feet or lower. The air is smooth and once again the view is stunning. Miles and miles of swampland meet the salty waters of the Gulf in this desolate, unforgiving piece of earth. Everglades National Park lies to the east and a place called Northwest Cape lies directly south. We pass the aptly named Lostman's River and I wonder aloud how anyone could ever escape its clutches once entering. The river winds back and forth and has countless tributaries connecting to it. From the air, it simply looks like a maze. Rob pipes in, confirming many people did get lost in there during his smuggling days. But for some—it was worth it, as they eluded capture by the DEA.

It doesn't take long for Marathon Key to appear on the horizon. I stay low while Rob tunes in the airport frequency. There's no traffic this early, which is perfect. We continue toward the airport at two hundred feet. Once there, I cross the field and turn southwest toward Sugarloaf Shores Airpark. Rob has me climb to five hundred feet and then he contacts Key West Approach, telling them we just departed Marathon and intend to land at Sugarloaf. Of course he uses a fake tail number, and again I just have to laugh. I've busted more FAA regulations in the last few days than I have in my entire life as a pilot. Then again, rules and regulations haven't really had a place in my life lately.

It only takes a few minutes and I'm lining up for landing on Runway 10. Once on the ground I taxi to the parking area and shut the engine down. Don (the mysterious looking airport manager with a scar on his forehead) approaches. He quietly looks the plane over, and after an inordinate amount of time asks how it flew. Rob says, "fine" and points me toward the boat. I grab some luggage and disappear.

The go-fast boat that Rob picked me up in two days ago is exactly where we left it. I take a seat and breathe in a deep sigh of relief. I'm still in a deep hole, but I have reason for a little optimism. I did the right thing by going to Fort Myers to get the heat off my new friends in Key West. I didn't get caught. And I'm about to return to Ballast Key for a little R&R.

It seems like an eternity before Rob finally gets to the boat. He's carrying two bags of supplies and points toward a five-gallon can of gas sitting next to the airport office. I gladly retrieve it. It never hurts to have extra fuel on Ballast.

Rob starts the engines and we idle toward the open water. After a few minutes in the canal, he pushes the throttles to full power and suddenly G-forces glue me to the stand-up style seats. The boat moves swiftly over the open water, allowing us to make Ballast in less than twenty minutes.

We arrive, and Rob throttles the engines back, inching the boat close to the long dock walkway. I tie it off and we begin unloading my things. Rob's in a hurry today and wants to get back to Key West, so I set my bags and the supplies on the dock and tell him goodbye. He smiles, then waves and compliments my work in Fort Myers. I smile and thank him again. He says to expect a visit from him and Gavin in a couple of days.

I untie the boat, push him off, and wave goodbye as the throttles are once again pushed to full power.

CHAPTER 22

September 19, 2008 11:00 a.m.

After lugging fresh supplies, my few belongings, and my tired ass up the dock walkway, a profound feeling of laziness overcomes me. The extra food and fuel have me set for the next few days, so I take full advantage of the solitude and lay down on the front porch of my guest house. It's funny, but after the last few days Ballast feels like home and I find myself thinking of it as my own. I wonder if Rob felt the same way by the time his ordeal was over?

It begins raining. Torrents hammer Ballast for hours. The severity of the storm makes me understand why Rob wanted to leave Fort Myers so early. It feels good to be on the ground in this weather.

I decide to fire up the generator, contact Gavin, and watch some news. Gavin has little to say but I can tell he's glad we're back safely. He mentions that his maintenance man has taken care of a few things, which means Rob made it to the South Breeze and Gavin is happy to have him back.

When the news comes on, I watch intently for anything about my case. The national Fox channel mentions nothing. It's not surprising since the package I sent to Elena wouldn't have arrived until today. Although she's had my email for nearly twenty four hours, she hasn't had time to think much of this through. When the local Fox affiliate news begins, Elena does a short blurb at a traffic accident on I-95—and that's it. I shut everything down, light the grill and enjoy a good hamburger, some chips, and a can of green beans. It's nice to relax and have a meal.

The morning sun streaming through the window is a perfect alarm clock. For the first time in days, I roll out of bed and feel well rested. I start the generator and make some coffee. It's a cool, comfortable morning, so I sit on the porch and enjoy the view. I cast a line for some fish and head over to the main house to check on it. The backyard area leading to the lagoon is a mess from the storm. I spend a few minutes picking up the debris and continue my way to the house and do a quick walk through. I'd finished the Grisham novel I borrowed last week, so I leave it on the table after making sure everything is okay. Rob mentioned some areas that needed painting when he was here last so I carefully inspect for flaking paint. The areas are easy to spot so I decide to give them some attention over the next few days.

When I return to the guest house, the fishing line I'd tossed out was already bent over. I reel in a nice Redfish and happily prepare it for the lunchtime grill. I wonder how being here would feel under different circumstances. I dismiss the thought and dive into a delicious lunch.

As the day goes on, boredom sets in. I fight it by checking email. My spirits brighten when I see one from Rob. He's cut and pasted an email from Brett's attorney, Pete Hoyt, in Trenton. I scroll through it and smile when I realize Brett has been scouring the files I sent him and Pete a few days ago. I assumed he would, but I didn't know how quickly it would happen.

Brett has an interesting question. He wants to know who Nikki Marris is. This takes me aback. I just assumed he knew about the murder from the news reports. But I guess he hadn't put two-and-two together yet. Her signature appears on title work he found in a file I worked on for a townhouse complex in upstate New York. According to Brett, there were only two people in the Northeast office that signed title work, and she wasn't one of them. This isn't the only thing he finds troubling. It also strikes him as odd that she signed off on one of his files in the same complex a few months earlier. He's adamant he wouldn't have noticed it because title sign-off was the last place his files went before closing. If they were signed off, he didn't even see them again. They would simply make their way back to the office for storage and future sale on the secondary market. So why would he look them over again if they made it through closing? Perplexed, I spend some time contemplating the same thing. Why would she be signing title work for files in New York? For that matter, why would she be signing title work for any file? She was an office manager!

Not sure what to think, I go back into my paper files and look for anything indicating Nikki had worked on them. After hours of searching, I find nothing. When I dig through my computer files and find the file Brett's referring to, I wonder aloud what fucking reason she would be signing title work for a New York real estate deal? But there it is, as plain as day. And I have no idea why.

I spend a few minutes writing an email back to Brett, thanking him for digging, and encouraging him to continue. I explain that Nikki was the wife of John Marris, the man I'm accused of murdering. I also explain that I'm stumped as to why her name appears on any file, and that I probably wouldn't have noticed either. I close the email telling him to hang tough, and that with a little luck we'll figure a way out of this mess. I send the email back to Rob and call it a day.

Chapter 23

September 21, 2008 7:00 a.m.

Another night of near comatose sleep has me bright eyed and alert shortly after the sun rises. The calm ocean breeze and the sounds of tropical birds are too inviting to ignore. I brew some coffee and take a seat on the porch. The solitude of this place is humbling. While it's nice for a few days, I'm realizing an extended stay here might become miserable. It's a funny thing about downtime. Not enough—you go crazy, too much—you go crazy. This motivates me.

The storage shed houses an abundance of maintenance items for use here on Ballast. I begin digging through the boxes of tools and supplies and immediately find paintbrushes, rollers, and trays. The aqua blue and pink colored house paint sits on the top shelves of the dusty old shed. I look at the rusty lids with a raised eyebrow as I pry open the one-gallon cans. Fortunately, the paint is fine. Taking advantage of the cooler morning temperatures, I walk to the main house and begin prepping the flaking areas for fresh paint.

While working, I keep wondering about the signatures Brett found. Did Nikki have more responsibility at Thrift Bank than

I knew about—than anyone knew about? I reflect on many interactions with her but still nothing makes sense. It's not like we engaged in pillow talk. We'd meet in the copy room or at my place for a quickie after work. Then she'd quickly make her way home to John. It was an empty relationship. At least for me.

I was so busy pushing paper, making sure all necessary items were present in any file I worked on, that it doesn't surprise me I never noticed. During those years, it was all about making more money. I guess that's the downside of working for big bonuses. In retrospect, I was probably oblivious to a lot of things. Brett and I may have been targeted for that reason. We were simply too busy to notice small details.

The day passes quickly as I scrape and paint. Once I've had enough, I sweep up the scrapings, close up the paint, clean the brushes, and head back to the guest house. An ice cold shower cools me off in time for the evening news.

With the generator running and the news blasting through the TV speaker, I decide to check email. To my delight, there are two from Rob. One is a response from Elena, and the other is from Pete Hoyt.

I read Elena's first. She looked through the package I sent her and has questions. She wants to know more about Nikki. She feels it's necessary to look into her marital relationship. She makes it clear that working for her husband at Thrift Bank complicates things. Seems smart to start there. After all that's come up over the last few days, I want to know more about Nikki too. She also comments that she's digging for info on Don Opitz. She mentions she has a contact with the Feds, but got nowhere with him.

Disappointed by Elena's email, I move on to the one from Pete Hoyt. Brett has found another Nikki signature. But this time it came from one of his files in Trenton and had nothing to do with any file in any community I ever worked on. This really baffles me!

After thinking it over, I start typing an email to Elena. I have no reason to hold back so I tell her everything that's transpired with Brett Bowers over the last couple of days. With Nikki's name popping up all over the place, it's possible she's deeper into this thing than I ever could have imagined—but how? She should be a low level player. Perplexed, I cut and paste the email and send it to Rob for delivery to Elena. I then type a short response to Pete Hoyt thanking him for his work. I again urge him to hold off on any plea arrangement regarding Brett. I just hope he doesn't jump the gun. If he does, Brett could wind up with a bad deal.

With the day winding down, the time comes for a radio call to Key West. The news from there is great as Gavin and Rob plan to visit tomorrow. Feeling better about things for the first time in a while, I crack open a beer and burn the remaining daylight with a fishing pole in hand.

Chapter 24

September 22, 2008 9:00 a.m.

A reverberating rumble greets my consciousness as I roll out of bed. It's much later than I usually wake up. Dark and stormy skies have a way of causing this. With nothing to do except wait on Rob and Gavin, I brew up a pot of coffee and take a seat on the front porch. Fortunately Rob threw a good novel in one of the supply bags we brought out a few days ago. It's one of those five-hundred page, small-print behemoths that take a century to read. It's a good thing too, as I have a lot of time to burn. It takes a few hours, but eventually the clouds begin to clear and the temperature rises. Sitting in the heat, and reading, don't go well together. So I set the book aside and take a walk.

For some reason, the stress of my situation is absent today. I feel calm and amazingly unconcerned. While I know nothing is resolved, it seems like I've at least garnered the interest of the reporter, which may give me a chance of turning things around. And knowing I've done what I can gives me a small sense of satisfaction, even accomplishment. And that strikes me as odd. I don't recall ever having a sense of accomplishment without a dollar sign attached.

Late in the day I see the flats-boat motor into the lagoon and under the camouflage netting. Rob's as boisterous as ever when he walks up to the porch and asks how I'm doing. Since I've had a few days of rest since our Fort Myers excursion, I'm honestly able to tell him I feel great. He gives me a snide look and asks, "Really?" Then he laughs and says, "Progress feels really good when you're in the shitter, doesn't it?" After a short pause and a blank stare from me, we bust out laughing. He's spot-on and we both know it. Gavin meanders up and nonchalantly comments that he doesn't even want to know what we're laughing about. Rob and I laugh even harder.

Gavin motions for us to unload the boat . We make our way to the lagoon and grab the bags of food and beer, and an unopened bottle of aged Jameson whiskey. Rob smiles and says Gavin wants a drink tonight. Gavin's a funny guy. His quintessential Key West look with the Hemingway hair and the beard are pleasantly disarming. He's such a good old man. One who wants none of life's stresses but also one who's willing to fight if necessary. Add a little criminal intrigue, and fortunately for me, it's a recipe he can't resist.

A mouth watering feast of steak and lobster is on the menu this evening. We light the grill just as the evening sky is turning bright red. Rob and I have already popped open a beer when Gavin breaks the seal on the whiskey. He throws the steaks on and orders Rob and I to prepare the salads and sides. We respond, "OK, Grandpa," and do as the old man says.

At dinner the conversation takes a turn I knew it would eventually take. Rob went to see Adriana at Dante's and showed her the pictures we took at the Lanai Kai in Fort Myers. Adriana believes one of them, the poor quality one, is the same guy who was nosing around Dante's. Rob smiles and says we're onto something here.

It seems even more unlikely these guys were law enforcement. If they were, they would have had backup in Fort Myers, and I would have been apprehended. I agree with him but am unsure whether to be happy about this or more concerned. One thing is sure: finding out who they are is priority one.

Rob then pulls out a printed email from Elena. She had sent it late day so Rob printed it before leaving Key West a few hours ago. She reports making a call to Dave Friedly, the Fed who contacted me when this whole thing blew up. She asked him about the Peter Johnson case. Elena explains how she went through the chain of command in getting to him. This way it shouldn't be evident she was in communication with me. She thinks it worked, but that he might suspect I contacted her. While this is worrisome, I knew it was a possibility.

She asked Friedly how closely he had looked into Nikki's past. She says she also asked if he thought a senior mortgage underwriter, a lower level position, could be into this so deep as to warrant a nationwide raid. Whether she was asking for her own need to understand or whether she's begun to believe in me isn't clear. But at least the questions are being asked. And that's good.

According to Elena, Friedly said very little but listened to what she had to say. She continued the email saying she informed him she would be doing a story on the mortgage meltdown and that the Thrift Bank case involving me would be included.

I'm pleased with how she handled him: It sounds like she gave herself good cover for nosing around. It might even be good if he suspects I contacted her because it opens a line of communication with the Feds. Maybe this helps. But if this guy's crooked, contacting him could be a disaster.

The dinner conversation continues as we walk to the main house and relax on the expansive wrap-around porch. Since I'm confident I've made a little bit of progress, I ask Gavin and Rob how they felt at this point in their dilemmas. Gavin gives me his old man smile and starts talking. Rob, never one to miss an opportunity to run his mouth, chimes in at the exact same time. We all laugh, but interestingly, Gavin keeps talking. He offers more about his troubles than he ever has. He reveals that he owned a large chain of coin-operated Laundromats. He was exhausted from long hours of work, and in dire need of some rest when he was approached by some wise guys with an irresistible offer. They would buy him out for full value and leave him with a half equity stake in the business. He would no longer manage it full time, but would still get paid a salary.

It sounded too good to be true—and it was. Dirty money was being laundered through the business, and the Feds eventually shut it down. He admits knowing it was going on but says that once it started, there was nothing he could do. Eventually he was pressed by the Feds to divulge information and was moved to Key West and given a new identity.

He smiles at me and says those were some very dark days. But he knew he had enough information to bargain with, and that kept him sane. He looks me straight in the eye and tells me I've got a good chance at clearing things up. He says this is a different time, and there would be no shame in turning myself in and hoping for the best. But not yet. He smiles, saying he thinks I'm close to breaking this thing wide open.

I sit in silence for a moment. Gavin's just admitted a certain degree of culpability in his ordeal, and he was able to bargain his way out. But he's right. It was a different time in history. Things were not as fast and the news wasn't on a twenty-four hour cycle in those days. It was probably much easier for the Feds to make deals for immunity.

Gavin keeps talking—or maybe it's the Jameson. Either way, I keep listening. He says at some point I need to start thinking about what I'm going to do when this thing winds down. I start laughing when he looks at me sternly and says, "When this is over, you'll never be the same!" While I agree with him, I tell him it's just too difficult to picture a future right now.

At this point, I have to ask both Rob and Gavin a question. Maybe it's the whiskey talking in me too. But I finally get up the courage to ask what I'll owe them when this is over. They just look at each other. Scared I offended them, I keep talking and hoping I'm not digging a deeper hole for myself. I tell them I know that hiding me isn't cheap. But when I can get money, I'll repay them all they're out. Rob confides that he asked Gavin the same question many years ago. Gavin smiles when Rob confesses this. He then says, "I knew Rob was a good egg when his concern wasn't only for himself." Rob pours more whiskey, says not to worry about the money, and downs a shot like it's water.

We've been sitting for an hour or so when I realize why Gavin chose the main house front porch for the evening festivities. It's dark now and the moon is beginning to peek above the horizon. Gavin smiles and says Rob and I need to start paying attention to the important things in life—like a good moon rise. We toast the important things in life with another shot of Jameson.

.

Chapter 25

September 23, 2008 6:30 a.m.

It's barely daylight when that damn rooster shows up again. It hasn't appeared in a while, and I'm pissed off it's here this morning. But at least Gavin and Rob will have to deal with it too. However, they don't seem to mind, as Rob's lying on the couch laughing and Gavin's still snoring. By the time I grab the pellet gun, load it and get to the door, it's gone. Now he's just screwing with me.

I roust Rob and put on some coffee. He grumbles at the early wake-up call but doesn't really seem to mind. The South Breeze needs some maintenance, and he wants to get an early start.

We sit on the porch talking. Since reading the email last night I feel the need to call Elena. Rob doesn't seem too concerned with the way I'm handling things now, so I'm guessing he and Gavin have begun to trust my judgment in fugitive matters. Nevertheless, we briefly discuss the call and agree that holding back my location is still necessary. I'm nervous because the more we talk on the phone, the greater the risk of slipping up and giving it away.

After taking in a nice sunrise, I go into the house, roust Gavin, and pull out the satellite phone and timer. I sit down on the couch and dial Elena. The caller ID is blocked, which I'm sure is why she answers immediately. Who else would be blocking their number?

I simply say, "Hello, it's Pete," and that the clock is ticking. She quickly chimes in, commenting how full of personality I am today. I chuckle aloud.

I thank her for the email and compliment the way she handled Friedly. I tell her that the poor quality picture we sent her is the same man who was looking for me at another location shortly after this mess hit the news. She quickly replies, "Where was that?"

"Nice try," I snap back.

I continue, telling her there's no way he can be law enforcement because he would have had backup that night in Fort Myers Beach.

It worries me when she asks, "You have help, don't you Pete?" She continues by saying she needs more to work with. I tell her to sit tight, that I'm working on things from my end and I'll give her more when I have it.

I ask if she's contacted the Miami-Dade Police yet. "She says no, but plans to today." She mentions her internet searches on politicians in the housing industry. I'm encouraged when she says firmly, "I have full support to investigate this." I interpret this as the station foaming at the mouth for a juicy story about corrupt government. I hope I'm right.

I'm looking at the timer as she mentions leaving for Jacksonville in an hour. She wants to swing by my condo to talk to Lindsey, the condo manager, and see if the pictures I sent her are any of the guys who were nosing around my place. She adds that she wants to meet Nikki if possible. I pause for a moment, realizing how much effort a drive to Jacksonville takes. This pleases me, but the timer beeps, so I cut her off, telling her I'll call right back. "You're a pain in the ass!" She yells, as I'm hanging up.

Still laughing, I dial her right back. She smarts off again but we quickly get back to business.

Concerned about the conversation she had with Dave Friedly, I ask why she thinks he might have suspected we were in contact. She says because he sarcastically commented that she should know to call Miami-Dade first. I immediately understand, and in my mind, I'm sure Friedly knows.

She wants to know why I think Friedly might be crooked. I make a snap decision to tell her about my tryst with the New York girl, but am careful not to say where it happened. I tell Elena that a call from that woman when the story hit the news is the only way anyone could have known where I was. If she called in with my location and people other than the cops got that close to me, then someone is dirty. Elena pauses, then agrees, but asks: "What if the woman phoned into Miami-Dade and never called the Feds?"

This hadn't crossed my mind. I confess it's something to consider. But either way, it means someone in law enforcement is dirty—just maybe not Friedly. The timer beeps again, signaling I'm down to fifteen seconds. I tell Elena to be careful in Jacksonville and to look for a new email from me later today. As I'm hanging up I hear her say, "This story might just be bigger than you, Pete."

Puzzled with her last comment, I mention it to Rob. It baffles him too. He says he'll have to think on it. Gavin pipes in saying he hopes the story's bigger than me too. I guess in Gavin's mind it means getting out of this will be easier.

It's late morning by the time we finish breakfast and load a few things into the boat. Rob and Gavin wave goodbye as they're backing out for the ride back to Key West. I watch them motor away, and in no time boredom returns.

CHAPTER 26

September 26, 2008 5:00 p.m.

Several days pass with little or no news. Fox briefly mentioned the Thrift Bank debacle but reported nothing new. Thankfully, the iPod is charged so I can at least listen to music to relieve the boredom. I sent Elena an email the day after Gavin and Rob visited. I gave her detailed information about the files that Brett found Nikki's signatures on. Since she has no idea of my rising suspicions about Nikki, I hope this points her in Nikki's direction. Frustrated because I haven't heard back from her, and knowing she's been in Jacksonville, has me pacing the island wondering what's going on. I hope today brings answers.

Late in the day, I get an email from Rob. It's a cut and paste from Elena earlier this morning. She reports chatting with Lindsey at my condo complex. Apparently Lindsey opened up to her, told her about the men who were looking for me. She said there were three that came before the police, and she identified the man in the shitty picture as one of them. She also claimed he had "beady-blue eyes." She thinks they may be the ones who kicked in my door. She said the police came a couple of days later and the maintenance man opened my condo up for them. They spent hours searching the place but appeared to take little when they left. Maybe a box of papers, Lindsey thought. She said those men were Federal agents with ID badges to prove it.

I'm surprised to read that Elena spoke with Nikki. She told Nikki she's doing a story on the mortgage meltdown and wanted her story because of the destruction it caused in her life. Nikki agreed to talk but only as a footnote, and that she wouldn't appear on camera. Elena was happy because she only wanted some background information anyway. She says the conversation didn't amount to much, Nikki simply playing the bereaved widow. She told Elena her work at Thrift Bank consisted of keeping things organized, and managing loan originators who were pitching mortgage packages to prospective home buyers. She never mentioned signing title work.

Nikki said she occasionally rubbed elbows with upper management, but that was mostly at corporate functions while accompanying her husband John. Elena writes that when she asked about me, Nikki became evasive. She said I was a hard-working underwriter and was surprised when I quit the way I did. She was also upset that the files went missing, because a lot of closings would be delayed. She had no idea that a few days later, those deals in progress would never close. She didn't mention our affair, but I'm surprised to read she thinks I killed John, and hopes I'm apprehended soon.

That pisses me off! She knows damn well that I had nothing to do with John's murder, and even said so when I talked to her on the satellite phone!

The silver lining in all of this is that Elena showed up for the interview early. When she did, a car was leaving Nikki's house. She snapped a picture of the license plate because the man driving it seemed to be in a hurry, and Elena felt he didn't want to be seen at Nikki's house.

Elena has more. She called a beat-cop she knows with the Miami-Dade police department and had the license plate run on the car leaving Nikki's house. It's registered to a retired Miami-Dade detective. She wonders what business Nikki has with a retired cop. So do I.

I need to talk to Elena, so I grab the satellite phone and timer, and punch in her number. She answers immediately, demanding to know when I'm going to give the three-minute rule a rest. I ignore it and ask her who the retired Miami-Dade detective is. She plays coy for a few seconds before saying that it gets even better. "His name is Jeff Triplett," she says. "I ran a Google search on him. A picture I found looks very similar to the one you gave me from Fort Myers!" I'm nearly jolted from my chair. In a light-hearted tone that doesn't match what I'm feeling, she asks, "What's the matter? Cat got your tongue?"

I'm still trying to process this revelation when she suggests I call Dave Friedly. Since I'm still convinced someone in law enforcement was tracking my movements through either the cell phone signal in Miami or the bank ATM, I'm not willing to risk my ass. But I tell her this new information seems to diminish the chances that the crooked cop is Friedly.

I ask her about the individual files Brett found with Nikki's signatures. Elena pauses and says, "Pete, it looks like Nikki is in this up to her eyeballs, and you need serious assistance from an FBI Mortgage Fraud Specialist."

"No shit genius," I tell her. "But I have two problems. Someone, and it might be this Triplett guy, is trying to kill me. Worse, he's connected to law enforcement, which means someone on the inside is helping him. So not only do I have that problem, there's also the matter of John Marris's murder being pinned on me. And that's not to mention all the Thrift Bank Mortgage fraud issues." I laugh and ask her, "Where the fuck would you begin, Elena?"

Silence on the line until I finally say, "What's the matter? Cat got your tongue?"

She tells me to make sure I watch the national Fox News tomorrow evening. I ask why and she snidely says I seem to be forgetting the three-minute rule. A cold shiver runs through me and she says, "Relax Pete, I'm not tracking you." She hangs up, leaving me deep in thought.

What the hell does all of this mean? I wonder aloud as I pace the confines of the shack. This news is encouraging, but I'm not sure what to do with it. And what does Elena mean about watching the news tomorrow? It must be something big if it's hitting the national news.

For now, all I can do is wait, hope, and think.

CHAPTER 27

September 27, 2008 6:30 p.m.

After an agonizingly slow day, Fox evening news begins with the headline: "Nine Senators and Five House members directly tied to Mortgage businesses." I'm breathing heavy with excitement as the report finally begins to air. Elena is front and center. Fox News seems to be treating this as a big scoop, and it looks like Elena did exactly what I hoped she would do— snag a big break.

I listen intently as she goes on about the different affiliations these guys have. One senator, a woman from California whom I've never heard of, is on the Senate Finance Committee with Bernie Frankel, and owns two large brokerages in California and Nevada. Another representative from New York is the largest stockholder and a board member of the largest homebuilder in America, Hatch Homes. She reports that all three of these politicians pushed for regulations allowing Fannie Mae and Freddie Mac to lower lending standards and increase allowable loan amounts. They then profited from the increased sales. The report concludes, saying that although no laws have been broken, serious questions of ethics violations exist.

Nothing was mentioned about the Thrift Bank Mortgage debacle in Elena's piece, which worries me. With all of the digging she had to do in order to piece together that story, why hadn't she tied Thrift Bank to it? Was there nothing to find? Am I missing something here?

After watching the story re-run in the evening cycle, I switch over to CNN and find they've picked up the story. Citing Fox News and their own sources, they report on even more links to businesses owned by congressional members with influence over government housing policy. It seems the bandwagon effect is underway. None of the networks want to look like they're missing a big story. I may have been onto something all along. But without a direct tie to Thrift Bank Mortgage, I don't know how it helps me. I head off to bed, uncertain about what to do next.

At dawn, the fucking rooster starts heckling me again. I grab the pellet gun and take a position near the end of the porch. I'm quickly rewarded with a clear shot. I hit it squarely in the breast, and it drops. I smile as I quickly clean and prepare it for lunch. Weeks of trying to kill that fucker should make the taste of success sweet.

I'm amazed at how a simple victory lifts my spirits. Reflecting on last night's news, I can only hope that similar progress is coming my way.

The morning news is even more intense. CNBC has picked up the story and the internet is abuzz with sleuths all over the country digging up anything and everything on our wonderful government leaders. There are so many ethics issues it's hard to keep up with them.

Feeling much better than I did when our last call ended, I decide to call Elena. I have no doubt she's expecting a call and she probably wonders why it's taken so long.

She answers on the first ring and immediately asks me what I think so far. I tell her it's great but ask why no connection to Thrift Bank? She sounds disappointed as she tells me she can't find one yet.

"This whole story is bigger than you, Pete," she says.

I snap at her, saying, "That's the second time you've said that! What do you mean?"

"What if this whole thing with Thrift Bank has nothing to do with what our politicians have been up to? What if you're simply the victim of a few fraudsters within your company, but there are no ties to big government?" she asks.

Honestly I hadn't even thought of that because of all the inside information someone would have had to have to track me. It just seemed so obvious with cops involved, and contributions to the Frankel campaign, that my problems were bigger than a one-business cover-up. Maybe not, but I'm not so sure just yet.

Elena keeps talking, saying she plans to continue trying to link Thrift Bank to the Frankels, or any other politician, but thinks that investigating Nikki is the only way to find out. She thinks Nikki is hiding something, and when she is thoroughly investigated, the key will lie somewhere with her. Elena again mentions Friedly, asking why I don't just talk to him.

I finally decide she's probably right. But there's no way I'm going to risk apprehension. Until this bullshit murder-rap is dropped, I'm not giving anyone a chance to get near me.

Walking around the island for a few hours seems to bring some clarity. It's time to make some tough decisions. I'm confident of what I need to do, but it still scares the hell out of me.

I use the radio to make a call to Gavin. I also email Elena via Rob. With nothing left for me to do, I spend the rest of the day finishing some touch-up painting on the main house, and cleaning up the landscaping around the yard and lagoon area. The place will be looking great when Rob and Gavin arrive tomorrow.

CHAPTER 28

September 29, 2008 4:00 p.m.

It's another late day arrival at Ballast for Gavin and Rob. In the past, this meant a big meal and a lot of booze, which is fine with me. But this time something's different. While they brought a lot of good food, there's no beer or whiskey in the cooler. Rob, never one to beat around the bush, hands me an email that arrived from Elena this morning.

In the email, Elena says she contacted Friedly and told him that someone was chasing me around Fort Myers recently. She also told him that the same guys looking for me there were nosing around in another location as well. Fortunately, she didn't know the location was Key West, which makes me really glad I didn't tell her.

She continues, saying she told Friedly that I believe the cops are crooked because the only way they could have known to look for me in any of these places was by tracking my movements electronically, or from tips hot lines (due to my picture being plastered all over the airwaves). Both of those likely required some level of assistance from a government entity.

She says Friedly is pissed off. He had just found out I was in Fort Myers a few days ago and had sent agents there to look for me. Apparently a tip came in, but he was a little late. This makes me chuckle. Rob sees the smile and mouths off, "Yeah, I like that part too!"

Elena also reveals that she told Friedly about the retired cop she saw at Nikki's house, and that she thinks there is more to this case than a pissed off mortgage underwriter murdering his boss.

Although I'd suspected this, it's the first time she's confirmed she has some belief in me. She finishes the email by strongly urging me to call him, and that she doesn't get the feeling that he's crooked. In fact, she thinks he's on his heels on this case because no one's talking to him.

Rob looks at me when I'm finished reading and says, "Let's eat!" Lost in thought for a few more seconds, I eventually smile at him and agree. The conversation takes a turn when they both congratulate me for shooting the rooster. We're all laughing when Rob tells me there will always be another one to take its place, as there are several flocks running around the island.

My mouth's watering when Gavin starts seasoning the thick, juicy rib-eye steaks he's brought. In his endearing and calm way, he motions for Rob and me to light the grill and scrape it clean. He says he doesn't want wild rooster contaminating his perfect slabs of red meat.

It doesn't take long to cook dinner. We're all seated on the porch to eat when Gavin looks at me and says, "So it's time, is it?" With mixed emotions, I nod yes and say, "I think it's time for me to move on."

I tell them I'm afraid that things might get too hot in Key West, and I don't want them to take any heat for it.

I also tell them I need to contact this Friedly guy and begin clearing myself. Even if somehow the mortgage fraud sticks, at least it looks like the murder-rap bullshit is looking flimsier.

Gavin pats me on the shoulder and says not to worry about any heat on him or Rob, and that if I feel I need to move on for purposes other than that, he's okay with it. He even thinks it might be a good idea to work with the Feds, especially in light of what Elena found out from Nikki.

At this point, Rob looks at me and says, "Don't fret Pete, I'm gonna give you some lessons on how to hide in plain sight!" After our trip to Fort Myers, I know exactly what he means. I start laughing when he tells me that the trash bag is going with me when I depart Key West, and I'll be an expert on how to use it.

Gavin begins to laugh, joking that he and Rob are training me to be the perfect criminal. Knowing they're right gets me laughing too. Ironically, when I was moving up in the mortgage business I spent a lot of time around people who were top producers. Simply stated, it's how I got good at handling mortgages. I guess this is no different.

With dinner winding down and no booze to speak of, Gavin looks me in the eye and says we are leaving Ballast tonight, and that I won't be coming back. He tells me he and Rob have a car and some money waiting at the South Breeze.

He says, "Saddle up, get this place locked down, and let's go to Key West for some drinks!"

It takes us all about an hour to walk the property and put everything away. I had a feeling this was coming down the pipe tonight, so I'd begun the process earlier in the day. The main house was already locked up and the equipment I'd been using was put away in the shed. Gavin commented on how nice the place looked and thanked me for my work.

"It's the least I could do," I tell him.

The sun's about to set on Ballast as we back the flats boat out of the lagoon and begin motoring towards Key West. I watch Ballast disappear as the lights in Key West begin shining over the water. Gavin and Rob notice my gaze and tell me not to worry, as my next trip to Ballast would be under much better circumstances.

"I hope you're right," I tell them.

Chapter 29

September 29, 2008 9:30 p.m.

We lumber along the southern tip of Key West for a few miles before Rob turns the boat toward the shore and idles up to the beach. Just as when I left, Rob and Gavin bring me back onto the island at Smather's Beach. We unload very few items. Gavin says not to worry, as Rob will bring everything back to the South Breeze after he docks the boat.

We hop out, and with wet and sloppy flip-flops, Gavin and I make our way to his old nondescript Pontiac. Within minutes the engine's fired up and the AC is cooling me for the first time in what seems like forever. Gavin chuckles as I aim one of the vents directly on my face. It's funny how we take for granted life's little luxuries. Air conditioning has never felt better, but it only takes five minutes until we pull into the South Breeze.

The South Breeze design is something right out of the '60s. The entrance is a one-lane driveway that sits between two buildings. Once past the first buildings, a few parking places sit to the right, a small swimming pool on the left, and a wide single story building with a metal roof borders the rear of the property. Thick, lush tropical landscaping is interspersed throughout, giving the place a nice island flavor, while also offering some privacy. The guest rooms have front doors that open onto a covered porch looking directly at the parking lot and pool. The buildings are all single story with white vinyl siding. Each front door has a plastic table with two chairs sitting next to it. There are four single rooms and thirteen double rooms. The place looks like something you'd find off of old Route 66, only it sits in the middle of a tropical paradise.

The Pontiac comes to a stop and Gavin hands me a key to room one. It's located in the back left corner of the property, opposite the room I stayed in when this whole fiasco began. I smile at Gavin because I know exactly why he put me there. It's the most secluded room on the property. He tells me to go in and clean up, that Rob will be there shortly with my things. "But," he adds, "Don't shave."

Within an hour Rob knocks on the door. I open it and he quickly brings in everything from the boat along with the big black trash bag full of appearance altering paraphernalia that he took to Fort Myers. By now it's nearly 10 p.m., and Rob says tonight is lesson one.

My black, 3-day island scruff is perfect for Rob's first lesson in disguises. Since my jet black hair was beginning to look scraggly and unkempt, it was perfect for Rob to train me. He hands me a diluted solution of bleach and hydrogen peroxide. He has me rub it over every hair on my head and face. Then he notices my arm and leg hair and has me do the same to those.

After an hour or so, he hands me several contact lens cases and carefully shows me the color-coded markings on the back of each. Tonight's is blue. He says since my eyes are brown, I should use this when my disguise is either a blond or a brunette. He says to use hazel when I pose as a redhead. Since I've never worn contact lenses, I haven't the slightest idea how to put them in. It takes a frustrating hour but finally I succeed. Rob laughs and tells me it gets easier with practice. I grumble but know it's a necessary skill.

Rob's attention to detail is not surprising. As much as he seems to bumble through life with a nonchalant attitude, he's very precise about some things. His experience is evident.

Next he hands me a small case with at least 15 different pairs of glasses. Some are to make you look older, some younger, and some trendy. He briefs me on which ones work well with tonight's costume. I shake my head, laughing, as he chooses the best pair.

He takes me into the bathroom and pulls out a scar kit. He carefully places one on my lower left arm. He says it draws attention away from my face and will be a trait someone will remember, further clouding their memory of me. Smart thinking.

He pulls out an assortment of hats. He says always wear the hat most common for a particular area. In the case of Key West, a nondescript ball cap. Tourists wear them all over the island.

We continue the disguise lesson as he coaches me on what to wear. Once again, it's all about blending in. Shorts and worn out T-shirts are best in Key West unless you're headed for serious nightlife areas, in which case you would dress up to blend in with the nightclub crowd.

Since tonight is just about a few drinks in an old locals hangout, Rob isn't too concerned. This relaxes me. If Rob and Gavin aren't worried, I'm not.

It's around midnight when we finally leave the South Breeze. We hop into Gavin's old Pontiac and turn right onto Simonton Street and head north toward the main tourist area in Key West.

We pull into a residential driveway right around the corner from a place called the Bull Bar. I comment about getting towed, and Rob just rolls his eyes. Then I get it. They must know the owner.

When we get out, Rob and Gavin tell me that I'm to walk north on Duval Street until reaching Greene Street, where Sloppy Joe's sits. I'm then to turn right, and I'll see a place called Guy Harvey's on my left. I'm to sit at the bar and they'll be along shortly.

That eerie feeling I had in Fort Myers is descending on me as I walk down the street. This time I don't want to be recognized so I'm looking closely for any signs that might mean trouble. It doesn't take long to realize that no one even notices me. After a few blocks of walking, my confidence rises dramatically.

I nonchalantly stroll into Guy Harvey's and sit down at the bar as instructed. The place is open air with a perfect view of Sloppy Joe's across the street. There are a lot of people moving around on the street and a band is playing at Sloppy Joe's—clearly audible from where I'm sitting.

The bartender heads my way and I order a beer. Within minutes Gavin and Rob enter the bar and sit down a few chairs away. I say nothing to them. I sit quietly for a few minutes when, as Rob is talking to the bartender, he introduces himself to me and says hello. The bartender is talking to Gavin and I can tell they know each other. Gavin then introduces himself to me and the bartender follows suit.

All of a sudden they start asking me questions about who I am and where I'm from. It hits me like a sledgehammer, because I hadn't remotely considered a story to tell since the plan, in my mind, was only to sit and enjoy Gavin and Rob's company. But right then I realize why we're out. I'm about to go out on my own, and I'd better have a good story to tell strangers. One that's believable and one I can remember. Why hadn't I thought about this?

Recovering from my hesitation, I decide to have a little fun with them. I politely tell them I'm from Broken Arrow, Oklahoma, and I'm here on a business trip. They ask me what kind of business. I hem haw around the question, stalling. It makes them dig harder, working to get an answer. When I confess that I sell battery-operated toys to adult bookstores, they bust out laughing and say, "Only in Key West!" The bartender laughs, saying someone's gotta sell them.

After a couple more beers, the conversation dies down. Rob and Gavin head out and a couple of minutes later I pay my tab and leave too. I walk south on Duval Street back toward the car, passing Rick's Tavern, Irish Kevin's, and several other Key West favorites. Within a few minutes I make it to Gavin's car, hop in and ask them if they need any sex toys?

Both of them frown, calling me a dipshit for using that story. They inform me we'll be working on a reasonable life history tomorrow. I can sense their displeasure but am so tired I don't care. A silent five-minute ride to the South Breeze, and the day draws to a close.

Clean sheets, air conditioning, and a hot shower have never felt so good.

CHAPTER 30

September 30, 2008 10:00 a.m.

It's around 10 a.m. when a knock at the door wakes me from a deep sleep. I roll around in the bed for a minute, trying to regain my senses. It's Rob, which is no surprise. I open the door and he's holding coffee and a plate of Cuban pork from Ana's Cuban Café across the street. Still wiping the sleep off of my face, Rob sits down and goes into his Robnoxious mode. He's wide-awake and excitedly telling me about a bed race we're going to participate in. He can hardly contain himself. I'm baffled. I have no idea what he's talking about.

I sit down at the table, and begin drinking the coffee he's brought. Finally, he slows his talking down enough for me to comprehend. From what I can gather, Key West has a rolling bed race down Duval Street once a year. It's an annual celebration of Key West independence and funds raised from the race go to the fight against AIDS. It begins to dawn on me that we're entered in the race.

As I eat, Rob leaves but returns quickly with two trash bags and a few dresses. My stomach churns as I realize what this means.

Rob just starts laughing and says, "You'll have no worries of being recognized today Petey!"

When I'm done eating, Rob goes into full costume dress mode. The only relief I get is that he's playing dress-up along with me today. Apparently the tradition is teams of three dress up in drag and race a bed with wheels down Duval Street. The winning team gets a $200 bar tab at a place called Bobby's Monkey Bar. Rob says it's great fun and a big tradition here in Key West.

Rob tells me not to worry about cleaning up or shaving. He hands me a dress, a large pair of ladies flats, and a wig of '80s style big hair. He then tosses me a pair of ladies sunglasses large enough to cover half of my face. When he whips out a pre-stuffed bra, I nearly double over laughing. While my stomach turns at the thought of dressing in drag, I crack up knowing there's no chance of anyone recognizing me today.

It takes a couple of hours to eat and dress. The shoes are uncomfortable, the makeup sucks, and the perfume is disgusting.

Around noon Gavin knocks on the door. He's laughing from the minute he steps in. He's seen Rob dressed like this before, but not me. He winks at me and says, "Hi sweetie." I wink back and ask if he's ready to watch us win the race.

He breaks out a flask and says, "No, but I'm ready for a shot, and I'm sure you are too." He's right. Within minutes the Jameson whiskey is flowing.

We walk out of the motel headed for the north end of Duval Street where the race begins.. Rob and Gavin have made arrangements with a friend of theirs to have our rolling bed ready. Just before we get to the street, Gavin asks lightheartedly, "Are you beginning to understand the blending-in concept?"

I am, and immediately tell him so.

With a raised eyebrow he looks at me and curtly quips, "Use the same concept when you tell someone about yourself. In other words, "Petey," give people a vanilla story so they won't remember you!"

I make it clear that I understand.

He cuts up saying, "Enjoy the day, Pete. No one will be the wiser!"

We cut over to Duval Street and walk north all the way to Schooner Wharf. When we arrive, there's a big sign reading: "Welcome to the Conch Republic—We succeeded where others failed!" The Bed Race is part of a daylong celebration commemorating the day when Key West seceded from the United States due to Border Patrol checkpoints on the only road in and out of the Florida Keys. It was 1982, and illegal immigration from Cuba was peaking. Eventually the roadblocks were removed and the hubbub died down. But by then, Key West, now known as the Conch Republic, had earned its place in American folklore.

When we arrive, an old friend of Gavin's named J.R. greets us. He has a queen-sized bed complete with large bicycle size tires, a rear brake, and handcuffs in four places to secure the man riding on the bed. He laughs when he sees Rob and me dressed in drag. Rob introduces me as Joe, a friend of his from Miami. Gavin shares another shot of Jameson just as we saddle up and prepare for the race.

The wharf is packed with revelers. I had no idea of the history of what I was walking into. I'd begun to understand the rebel roots of Key West, but it really hit home when I began to understand some of the recent history of the island. Pirates, non-conformists, witness-protection participants, illegals—you name it—Key West has it. These people are proud of their heritage, and it shows. It's barely 1p.m. and the island is already alive with celebration.

The announcement came for the bed racers to line up. J.R. climbed onto the bed and I could only laugh as Rob and I hand-cuffed him to it. I noticed that other racers were only loosely tying their riders on, but J.R. was adamant about not being thrown from the bed. I understood why when he quipped about not tearing up the dress he was wearing. This guy enjoyed dressing in drag. Rob noticed when I caught on and it made him laugh too.

When the gun goes off signifying the start of the race, the crowd goes wild. I push as hard as I can and so does Rob. The crowd lining Duval Street went wild. It's hilarious. We're all running into each other, and there's numerous bed wrecks. One bed looked like it wouldn't even finish the race. Rob and I are laughing so hard we can barely move the bed.

Out of nowhere, I suddenly see Rob get a fierce look in his eyes. He forcefully tells me to look the other way and haul ass. He's serious and I don't know why. I do as he says, wondering what just happened. We push and pull, grunting and groaning until finally making it to the finish line. We nearly win the race. The crowd is going wild as Rob orders me to return to the South Breeze with Gavin immediately.

Gavin had left the starting area of the race a few minutes before it began. Not surprisingly, I see him standing at the corner of South and Duval as soon as Rob tells me to leave. His eyes dart toward Gavin, and Gavin instinctively knows what to do. We move into the crowd, making our way past Ana's Cuban café, turning left onto Simonton Street, and finally ducking into my room in the back corner of the motel.

Within 20 minutes, Rob arrives. He has fire in his eyes when he tells Gavin and I that he's sure he saw the beady blue-eyed guy in the crowd. Luckily the guy didn't notice us. He's concerned and so am I. Why is this guy back in Key West? None of us have a clue.

Rob doesn't stay long. He leaves, telling me to stay put until he gets back. I turn to Gavin and wonder aloud if this is the same guy Elena saw named Jeff Triplett—the retired Miami-Dade cop.

CHAPTER 31

September 30, 2008 2:00 p.m.

Gavin leaves the room shortly after Rob. I take off my fancy dress and put on a pair of old jeans. The other female attire I simply throw in the corner and immediately head to the bathroom to remove the mascara I'd applied before the bed race.

I turn on the TV, and as if it were reading my mind, Fox News Channel is cued up, blaring at full blast. I take a seat on the bed, lower the volume and just sit. I wonder why this Triplett guy is still looking around Key West for me. What would bring him back here? And if it was him at Nikki's place, how were they connected?

Hours later Rob and Gavin walk in with no warning. I'd dozed off so I jump and flail when they roust me. I can tell they're in a serious frame of mind. Rob says that the guy we believe to be Triplett confronted Adriana again. He thinks the description of Triplett from Adriana, the grainy photograph from Fort Myers, and his sighting of the guy today confirms it's him.

He continues though, saying he's going on a hunting expedition in Key West for the next couple of days. He wants a perfect picture of this guy and says somehow, he's going to get one.

I wander around the room trying to regain my wits, and I feel anger building inside me. I realize I have to leave Key West now. The longer I'm here, the more everyone who's helped me is at risk. I tell them I've got to go, and it's apparent we're all thinking the same thing. Gavin hands me an envelope. Rob tosses me a set of car keys, but I cringe when he hands me a small case holding a .38 revolver. He notices my reaction and says to relax, that hopefully I'll be able to throw it into the Gulf when this thing's over.

It's a beautiful day in Key West but it's too risky to go out in daylight with Triplett roaming around. I hole up in my room and begin organizing my things. I slip out of the room briefly to use the motel laundry machine and spend the rest of my time researching places I might stay. Rob and Gavin suggest making camp in Tavernier or Florida City. Tavernier is a small town in the Upper Keys, which provides easy access to the mainland. Florida City is a dumpy little town just before you reach the Keys. Both offer me access to highways going to the west coast of Florida or the I-95 corridor. After weighing a lot of options, I decide on Tavernier. At least it's still in The Keys and life sucks a little less with an ocean view.

As the day presses on, I make a list of what I'll likely need in the coming days. It's past time to make copies of the paper files Rob and I recovered on U.S. 1. I call Rob and ask for a cheap scanner I can hook to my laptop. Within an hour it's delivered. I spend the next few hours scanning every document we found that morning. I still have no idea what these files have in them, but I'm about to let both Friedly and Elena have them. My give-a-shit meter just isn't working anymore.

In the evening, Rob shows up with hot sandwiches from a local sub-shop. Gavin joins us and we chat for a bit. Rob spent the day hopping from bar to bar in search of Triplett but had no luck. He plans on spending the day at Dante's tomorrow with Adriana. Hopefully he'll hit pay dirt.

Before Rob and Gavin leave, I ask Gavin to use the copy machine in the South Breeze front office. Rob and Gavin both volunteer to help. I gladly accept and then ask them to keep a full set of the copies in a safe place just in case. Gavin readily agrees.

CHAPTER 32

October 1, 2008 5:30 a.m.

The morning arrives quickly. I hop in the shower, dress, and begin applying a disguise. I leave my unshaven island scruff, re-dye my hair blond, and reapply the nasty looking scar to my lower left arm. I'm careful not to get carried away, knowing this disguise will need to be reapplied every day until I leave Tavernier. Anyone I meet will begin to remember me based on this appearance. Once the disguise is complete, I choose a couple pair of suitable glasses and head out to the car.

It's just after 6:30 a.m. when I leave my room. I begin loading the trunk of a nondescript early-2000 model Honda Civic. The paint job is a slightly worn gold color that seems as common as the car itself. Gavin walks over and motions me back to my room. He hands me an envelope. He tells me to use it only if necessary—as a last resort—and to not even look in it unless things get really bad. Perplexed, I agree. Then he hands me several pre-paid cell phones he'd had shipped from different places around the country. He says to use them as needed. Finally, he gives me the satellite phone I had on Ballast Key. He says to use it carefully, as it may have been compromised already.

Just as Gavin and I are finishing up, Rob comes bouncing around the corner. He has a stack of papers, all neatly placed in a manila folder. It's the email addresses and passwords of the bogus accounts he and I have set up to communicate over the last month. He makes sure I understand this process needs to continue in order to keep in touch.

After a few more pleasantries, we all shake hands. After everything they've done for me, I struggle to say something that feels appropriate. I end up thanking them for everything. They simply smile and say they'll be expecting to hear from me.

The drive off of Key West feels eerie. Knowing I'm headed into the unknown again has me on edge. If not for having a little backup in Gavin and Rob I'd be lost. I've relied heavily on them and today I feel alone—really alone.

The drive up U.S. 1 is uneventful. I stop for gas just to battle my jittery nerves. I continue driving until I arrive at a place called Keane Camp. It's an RV park with a small motel at mile marker 104. In the Keys, all businesses give directions and advertise based on mile marker numbers. Since there's only one way in and one way out of the Keys, it makes sense. The numbers are in ascending order beginning in Key West at marker 0 and ending at 115 where Monroe County meets the southern tip of Florida. Florida City where the Florida Turnpike links up is a little farther north at mile marker 127 in Dade County.

Just before checking in at Keane Camp, I open the first envelope Gavin had given me back at the South Breeze yesterday. I had planned on using a fake name when I checked into the new motel and hoped I could avoid showing identification by using cash. Gavin was a step ahead of me. In the envelope were two forms of identification. One is a Florida driver's license under the name of Bernhard L. Motz from Fort Myers, Florida. The other is a blood donor card under the same name and address. I laugh softly for a moment. I should have known he'd handle that detail. I just figured the envelope had a stack of cash in it. Fortunately, it included one of those too. Now I'm wondering what is in the other envelope he told me not to look at unless things were really getting bad.

I take a few minutes to memorize the information on the driver's license, and then write down a fake tag number for the car before entering the Keane Camp reception office. It's an old building, one that seems to have seen it's share of tropical storms. I'm hoping the rooms are at least clean, but since the place is off of the main highway and on the water, it's perfect, clean or not.

An older woman is at the reception desk. She smiles kindly at me, and asks if I have a reservation. I tell her no, wondering how many people actually make a reservation at a place like this. She then asks what type of room I'd like.

"A single room in a quiet area," I tell her.

She does her thing with the computer for a moment and then pulls out a map showing me where the room is on the property. I'm pleasantly surprised. I can park the car right in front of the door, and the rear wall of the room has a sliding door walking out to a deck overlooking the Gulf. I fill out the guest card, carefully using my new alias, give her the license plate number for the car, and pay her for a week in cash. Eying the scar on my left arm, she tells me to enjoy my stay.

It's still early in the day when I settle into my new digs. The room is small but clean. The décor is typical island flare. Tile floors, beach pictures, bamboo bedposts, and a view of the Gulf round out the ambiance. Fortunately a mini-fridge sits in the corner. I fill it with several items I'd purchased while gassing up the car.

I sit down at the bamboo desk facing the water and open my laptop. I want to check the Internet for any new news on the story. The hotel TV offers the Fox News Channel, so between both I'm up to date in no time. Several more senators and a few representatives have been connected to various housing related businesses. There is now speculation that some will be forced to resign. It's turning into one of the largest scandals of my generation.

I log into one of the email accounts Rob and I plan to use. I fire off a short email letting him know I'm settled in and looking forward to a clear picture of Triplett.

Struggling with the risks I'm about to take, I pick up the satellite phone and dial Elena. Her line goes directly to voice mail, which pisses me off. I simply tell her we need to meet and hang up. It's approximately 1p.m. and with nothing left to do except wait, I unpack a few things and take a nap.

CHAPTER 33

October 2, 2008 7:00 a.m.

My first morning at Keane Camp is nice. The in-room coffee maker works perfectly, and the donuts and banana I bought yesterday hit the spot nicely. The view of the gulf is relaxing and I feel well rested. Even the bed gets an A+ for comfort.

After a few minutes in deep thought, I open my laptop and check email for a note from Rob. Pay dirt! There's an email with an attachment. My excitement turns to fear as I begin reading. The good news is we finally have a clear picture of Triplett. It's definitely the same guy from Fort Myers. The picture was taken mid morning yesterday at a little breakfast dive on the Wharf in Key West. The problem is Adriana missed her evening shift at Dante's and never called in. Rob is worried. Adriana would never do that. My relaxed feeling evaporates, replaced by a sick feeling at the thought of what might have happened.

I don't have a usable number for Rob, so I make the snap decision to call the South Breeze. When Gavin answers, I say, "I'd like to speak with your maintenance man please."

Gavin responds, "I'll have to give him a message."

Knowing Gavin recognizes my voice, I simply leave the number to the phone I'm using.

For the rest of the day I wander aimlessly around Keane Camp waiting for a return call from Rob. Eventually, I walk across U.S. 1 to a little dump bar called the "Stinky Fish," and proceed to drink myself into oblivion. The bartender is an old guy who's only comment to me is how quiet I am. I say nothing, my only communication to him is to motion for another beer. After several hours, I decide it's time to return to my room. I pay the tab, tip the bartender and walk back across the street to Keane Camp and pass out.

It's barely midnight when I wake up with a pounding headache. It's the kind of headache that makes you consider never drinking again. Unfortunately the drinking did nothing to relieve my fear of what may have happened to Adriana. I pace a while, lay back down, pace a while, and lay back down again. All to no avail. Sleep is just not going to be possible. I'm not sure what feels worse, the hangover or the thought that something has happened to her.

As the sun begins to edge over the horizon, sickness and fear are replaced by anger. These guys are never going to stop, and eventually they're going to hurt everyone who has ever helped me. There's only one thing I can do and it scares the shit out of me. I've got to go after these guys or this mess will never end. I'm fed up with running.

I sit for a while, racking my brain trying to figure a way to lure these assholes to me. After a while it becomes clear there's only one way to make that happen and I'll have to be the bait.

Finally, the phone rings. It's Rob, but he doesn't have much to say. He tells me Adriana is still missing and that he looked for her all day yesterday. He says he would have called but he had nothing to tell me. He plans to continue looking today.

It's then I tell him I'm working on a plan. I tell him where I'm staying, the room number, the layout, you name it—Rob now knows it. I also tell him I'm going to need some help, the violent kind, and ask if this evening is too quick. I continue, saying if this works, Triplett will have no need for Adriana.

He's surprised by how quickly I want to move, but I can tell he's become comfortable with my thinking. And he also knows if we're going to help Adriana, we're going to have to move fast. I finish the conversation by telling him it will be dangerous and there's no guarantee I'll get out alive. But if anything happens to Adriana, I couldn't live with myself anyway. He seems to sense my urgency. He says to check email later in the day.

Next, I grab the satellite phone and dial Elena, my finger stabbing the keys. Fortunately she answers. Wasting no time on bullshit, I tell her it's time we meet, and it needs to happen now. I ask where she is.

She replies, "West Palm."

"Good," I tell her. "Get in your car and meet me at the Last Chance Saloon in Florida City in 3 hours." I hear her grumbling and pushing back as I tell her I'll have the paper files, and that I need a favor.

"Someone I care about is in trouble and if you fuck me on this, something terrible might happen."

She begrudgingly agrees. I tell her to take one of the back corner booths and that I'll get there shortly after she arrives. The call lasts less than 2 minutes. I've now got very little time to prepare for what will likely be the most dangerous day of my life.

I stuff two flash drives and two of the cell phones in my pockets. I carry the paper files and the case with the .38 to the car. For the first time in my life I'm glad I have a gun. But it's a hollow, sick kind of feeling, because I think I'll really need it.

The Last Chance Saloon is at the south end of Florida City. It's called that because it's the last bar before entering the Florida Keys. Back when drinking and driving wasn't a crime, Key West revelers were known to begin their party there, making the 127 mile drive to Key West in a better mood than I'm in now.

The drive north to Florida City takes only 45 minutes. Across the street from the bar is an old gravel parking lot with an exit onto a small street running parallel to U.S. 1, offering exits going north or south. I'm not sure if I'll have to run after this meeting, but I like having an option.

I park and slip into the palmetto bushes on the south end of the lot. Hiding there gives me a perfect view of the bar. If anyone out of the ordinary enters, I'll see them. "Ordinary" being anyone who looks like a local drunk. It's not even eleven.

Mosquitoes and gnats swarm me as I wait for Elena to arrive. A few cars pull into the bar. A few tourists pile out. Nothing seems amiss. About 45 minutes later, I see Elena enter. I watch for another 20 minutes making sure no one has tailed her. Things look clear, so I make my way across U.S. 1 and enter. It takes a few minutes for my eyes to adjust, but Elena is right where I told her to be. She looks even better than on TV.

There are some old and worn-out looking locals at the bar. A few tourists likely headed into the Keys for a short holiday take up a couple of the booths. It's barely noon but I order a beer to calm my nerves. I continue watching Elena for a few minutes trying to figure out if anyone recognizes her. No one does and no one seems to recognize me either. The scar on my arm helps me blend in. I finish the beer and head to the men's room before making my way to Elena's booth.

Sliding quickly into the booth, she startles. "What's the matter? Cat got your tongue?" I ask. She forces a smile and quips, "Yeah, I've never sat at a bar with a felon before." It pisses me off until she wryly smiles at me. I can tell she doesn't believe it. I thank her for her help and we sit in silence for a moment until she finally says, "OK Pete, what's up?"

I tell her about Adriana and of my suspicions that the guys from Fort Myers may have kidnapped her. I'm afraid of what they'll do to her. Adriana has no idea where I am, but these guys may think she does. I have to find them, and I have a plan. Finally, I tell her, I'm sick of running.

"Where are they? And where have you been hiding?" she asks.

"You don't really need to know that," I say.

She looks at me as if I'm crazy, finally saying, "Maybe you're right." Then she adds, "What do you want me to do?"

I tell her to call the Miami-Dade Tips Hotline anonymously and tell them she saw me at a place called Keane Camp in Tavernier. She's speechless. Silence fills the air until she asks if that's truly where I'm staying.

When I tell her yes, she asks why I would turn myself in. I tell her I hope Friedly is a good cop. I think that the connection she made between Triplett and the Miami-Dade police is plausible. If it's Triplett getting information from someone at Miami-Dade, he'll get the information before Friedly and come looking for me in Tavernier. With a little luck, they'll dump Adriana. I'll know they're coming, and I'll have a chance to capture or kill them.

She says, "You're no killer Pete, you're all of 160 pounds soaking wet—and you think you can stop them?"

I tell her I'll have help, and that it's the only way I can be certain they're stopped. I tell her if I'm right about Triplett, I'm only solving one problem. I'll still have Friedly and the mortgage fraud charges following me. But at least I'll only have the Feds to deal with and they aren't trying to kill me.

Elena sits quietly. Finally she asks where the files are. I reach into my pocket and hand her the two flash-drives. "One for you and one for Friedly." I tell her. "I have paper copies in a car across the street."

"Originals?" she asks.

"No," I tell her. "I'm saving those for Friedly."

"OK," she says, "but you'd better not be bullshitting me, Pete."

She sits quietly again, thinking. I lean back in the booth looking at her, trying to figure out what's going through her mind. Eventually, with a vexing look on her face, she says, "There's no way I'm going to get involved in this Pete. You'll have to figure out how to get this call made without me. But I'll do you one small favor. I'm going to keep quiet about this little escapade long enough to see if you're right. That's the only favor you're going to get from me."

She then smiles while looking me in the eyes. I sit speechless for a few seconds, finally chuckling to myself, thinking this is the kindest "fuck you" I've ever heard.

I smile back and say, "Fair enough, I'll make the call myself."

An awkward silence lingers until for some reason we both start laughing. I sense a soft side to her but realize she's not ready to travel down that road. My palms are sweating, something I haven't felt since I was a kid. I wonder for just a minute about what it would be like if we were just two people having a beer. But there's no time to indulge my fantasies.

I tell Elena that there's a clear picture of Triplett headed her way.

"What do you want me to do with it?" she asks.

"Get it to Friedly. Maybe he can help," I reply.

We again sit in silence for a moment when finally Elena looks at me and says, "You really don't have anything to do with this do you?"

"Yeah, I do. I screwed around with my boss's wife and used her as a pawn when I quit my job. By making out with her and being sure to do it when I knew John would catch me, I inadvertently became heavily involved—only as a bigger pawn than I took Nikki for. I thought I was just screwing over John. I hated the guy but had no idea what was going on behind the scenes at Thrift Bank. They might have tried to pin the mortgage fraud on me regardless of my affair with Nikki. But quitting my job in such a juvenile way probably gave Nikki and Triplett the perfect opportunity to kill John and make it look like I did it. I made a huge mistake."

Silence again fills the booth until she finally busts out laughing, saying, "Pete, you must have been really sick of your job!"

We both start laughing, almost uncontrollably. Knowing I've lost all control and will likely get busted by the Feds or killed by Triplett and his henchmen seems to have given me a sense of gallows humor. But I've always heard you should fear the man who has nothing to lose, and that is certainly the case with me. I hope that my desperation means big trouble for this Triplett guy.

"C'mon," I tell her, "It's time to go. I've got a call to make."

"Where are the files?" she asks as we walk into the dirty gravel parking lot. I point across U.S. 1 and tell her to park on the south end of the lot. I walk across the street, walk into the palmettos and reappear at her passenger side door. She opens it and I toss the trash bag full of files into the car. She lightly grabs my arm, smiles at me, and says, "I hope to see you again, Pete." Disarmed, I smile and say thanks.

CHAPTER 34

October 3, 2008 2:00 p.m.

As soon as I return to Keane Camp, I use the laptop to send Triplett's picture to Elena. Thinking back on our conversation at the bar, I realize she has a lot of options. I'm certain she'll do something. I'm just not sure what. It's possible the Feds will show up here at Keane Camp any minute. But I believe it's more likely Triplett and his guys will show up first. Hopefully not until I'm ready.

Next, I check for an email from Rob. He's quick today, which is a relief. He left a cell number for me, and he's specific about the time to call. He seems to be in no mood to mess around with emails.

It's 3 p.m. when I phone him. He answers on the first ring and asks, "What's going on?" I respond by asking if Adriana has turned up. He says no, and that he went by her apartment. She's not there and her purse and keys were left on the kitchen table. He says he hasn't been able to find Triplett either and he's been looking all day. After taking the picture, he tailed him for an hour or so until losing sight near a bed and breakfast called

Courtney's Place on Petronia Street. He thinks these guys might be staying in that area.

I give Rob my plan. I tell him that I'm going to call a tip into the Miami-Dade hot-line as to my whereabouts in a couple of hours, and that I'm gambling Triplett and his guys will get that information before the Feds. Hopefully they'll leave Key West in search of me. It's then I'm hoping they'll release Adriana, if they have her.

Rob offers an exasperated sigh and says I'm fucking crazy. But he's glad. I can hear it in his voice.

Then he says, "Pete, I'll watch the alley behind Courtney's Place and if they're staying in any of the bed-and-breakfast's along that alley, I should see them leave. Give me one of the cell numbers you have and keep the phone turned on this afternoon. With a little luck, I'll see them leave and give you a heads-up."

I tell Rob to use the one I'm calling from, as this is the only time it's been used. There's a brief pause in the conversation when he finally chimes in saying, " Pete, do what's necessary. Adriana's in serious trouble."

"OK," is all I can say.

Nothing more needed to be said. Rob knows I'm planning to kill this guy and anyone who's working with him. He and I know it's probably the only way I'm ever going to get rid of them—and most likely the only way to get Adriana out of their grips. So I sit in the Keane Camp motel room pondering murder. Knowing it's self-preservation, and possibly the only way I can help an innocent woman, doesn't make it any easier. Elena was right when she said I'm no killer. I'm not, but I realize I'm likely to become one.

With very little time to spare, I begin putting my plan into action. First, I pack a change of clothes, a few toiletries, and

Gavin's last envelope in a suitcase. I separate the items in the trash bags used for disguise. Some I'll need today and some a little later. I open the door to the room, walk to the car and carefully place all of it in the trunk.

Once I have the car loaded I sit down next to the phone near the bed, and with my nerves shot, I dial the operator and ask for an outside line. Within minutes I hear a woman answer, "Miami-Dade tips hot-line."

I muffle my voice with a wet washcloth and say, "I just saw the guy on Fox News that's wanted for that murder in Miami a while back. He's at a place called Keane Camp in Tavernier."

"How long ago did you see him?" the woman asks.

"About 10 minutes ago, and I'm sure it's him," I say. "Pete Johnson's his name, I think," I continue.

"Please stay on the line," the lady says.

I hang up and take a deep breath, knowing I just rained down a lot of heat on myself.

I dig around online for an FBI address where Dave Friedly would be likely to receive mail. I grab the original Thrift Bank files and head down U.S. 1 to a UPS store in Tavernier. In less than twenty minutes the original files are en-route to Friedly.

In the same strip mall as the UPS store there's a Kmart. I step in and quickly make my way to an aisle with signage. When I left Keane Camp, I noticed several cars sitting on the edge of U.S. 1 with "for sale" signs in the windows. They're all within fifty yards of my room. When I return to Keane Camp, I pull the Honda between two of those cars and place an identical "for sale" sign in the window. The car blends in perfectly; it's pointed toward the highway, effectively hiding it in plain sight.

Keane Camp is an interesting place. The clientele varies from older folks, to families, to boaters coming down from Miami and Ft. Lauderdale. There's a nice Tiki Bar on the boat dock overlooking the water, and according to the lady running the operation, they have live entertainment every night. She says the music brings in lots of locals and turns the place into quite a party. For my sake, I'm hoping it's a packed house tonight.

At this point it's been nearly four hours since Elena and I left The Last Chance. I'm guessing if she was going to turn me in she's already done it. If not, either local cops or Triplett and his thugs are en-route. Either way, the clock is ticking on my visitors—whoever they happen to be.

Fortunately the disguise bag has everything I need for a complete makeover. First, I get out the clippers and shave my head, leaving only slick skin. I apply a thin paste on my scalp, just as Rob had shown me a few weeks back, and attach a thin gray wig with a matching beard and mustache. At this point I retrieve the clothes bag and put on an old pair of boat shorts, a beat-up boating hat, and a pair of no-style glasses. Noticing my arm hair is not matching the wig and beard, I retrieve the hair coloring and apply it to my arms and legs. During this process, I remove the old scar I've been using since yesterday. Once my disguise is complete, I bag up the extra stuff and set it by the door.

The bed sits between the front and rear door of the room making it visible from either entrance. I begin stuffing sheets and towels into a pair of dirty pants and a shirt. I grab a pillowcase and stuff it, turning it into a round ball. Next, I retrieve an old wig and a hat out of the disguise bag. In no time, the bed has the appearance of a man sleeping in it.

I then crack the front and rear doors of the room, leave on a reading light and the TV, grab what's left of my things, and walk out of the room.

CHAPTER 35

October 3, 2008 8:00 p.m.

The sun's pretty low on the horizon as I nonchalantly walk toward the car. A thick strand of palmettos is conveniently located between the parking lot of Keane Camp and U.S. 1. I'm able to meander through the palmettos and pop out at the trunk of the Honda. I open it, place my last few items inside and disappear back into the palmettos.

I wander through the campground saying hello to a few guests, trying to see if they're noticing anything odd about me. Strange looks are nonexistent so I continue walking toward the bait shop. Once there, I buy a cheap lawn chair, a fishing pole, some tackle, a bag of stink bait, and, to calm my nerves, I grab a 24-ounce Heineken.

A few minutes later I'm set up with my fishing pole about 30 yards from the back door of my room. Approximately 10 yards further up the beach is a young couple. They're also fishing. What they don't know is, I'm hunting.

I've been expecting to hear from Rob ever since we hung up at 3 o'clock and finally the phone rings. Fumbling around my pockets, I finally get to it. He simply says, "Expect company," and hangs up.

I'm startled, perplexed, relieved, and worried all at the same time. I assume he means Triplett, but maybe not. Why such a short call I wonder? Is it possible Triplett's gang got Rob and that's why? No, I think, because he wouldn't be able to call me at all. I'm totally confused. I simply sit, acting like I'm fishing and wait.

The sun's beginning to set when the Tiki Bar band starts playing. People have begun to move around, making it more difficult to focus on anyone looking out of place. I'm guessing Triplett's gang knows this and is likely already here. I simply wait, watching the unlatched sliding door of my room, waiting for the inevitable arrival of someone wishing to make my life more of a hell than it's already become.

As the grounds fill with partiers, I blend into the surroundings even more. Several people walk by and say hello, not noticing anything odd about me. Then I see a guy walking toward my room on the rear sidewalk. The sidewalk sits atop a seawall just steps above the sand.

He's in a hurry. He passes the door, calmly looking at it, but continuing to move briskly. I move a little closer to the door, casually adjusting my fishing spot due to the incoming tide. I'm no more than 20 yards from the door when I see him. I freeze. Trembling with fear, I turn my head and watch out of the corner of my eye, never losing sight of the beady blue-eyed bastard.

By now it's dark. Lights line the dock, the sidewalks, and the front of each hotel room door, but they fail to provide even a semblance of good visibility. When I see him step into my room, I quickly make my move. With hands shaking and so much adrenaline pouring through my veins that my knees are weak,

I step in behind Triplett, shut the door while simultaneously pressing the barrel of the .38 to the back of his head.

"Don't move," I tell him as I shut the door. His hands slowly begin to rise when he quickly elbows me in the face. I point and fire as I fall back toward the wall. The sound is deafening. He slumps but manages to grab me by the throat, when out of nowhere a large heavyset Cuban looking guy steps out of the bathroom and grabs him, throwing him to the ground like a rag doll. The Cuban guy then looks at me, motioning toward the front door.

Dazed, confused, and in serious pain, I move toward the door. It opens and I look up to see Alvarez, the salvage shop owner from Miami. He grumbles a bit about getting me out of here when he's suddenly pushed into the room from behind by two thugs I can only assume are Triplett's guys.

With Triplett on the floor wounded, Alvarez's partner moves into the fray and a full-on fight ensues. The two men who pushed in behind Alvarez have guns drawn and another shot fires as Alvarez pounds one of the two men into oblivion. He drops and Alvarez turns his attention to the third man. Between him and his partner, Triplett's guys are pounded to within an inch of their lives and all of a sudden it's quiet. Triplett and his thugs lay wounded or beaten on the floor and I'm standing in the middle of a ransacked room wondering what the fuck just happened.

Alvarez closes the front door and his friends use zip-ties and ball-gags to secure Triplett and his men, casually kicking them for good measure. They begin scouring the room for anything that could possibly link them to the scene. Triplett is bleeding profusely from the bullet wound I administered, so Alvarez's friend does a quickie, makeshift bandage job on him.

I stand in the room looking around in complete amazement. I must look like a deer in the headlights when Alvarez simply says to me "We're leaving. Do what you want with them. Our work is done!" The door slams as they walk out.

I'm lost in the moment when survival instinct suddenly kicks in. There's no use in cleaning up anything linking me to this room. It won't take a genius to know I was here. Concerned about the noise that must have come from the gunshots, I peer out the front door of the room, glancing back and forth across the parking lot several times. I see nothing.

A queasy sick feeling envelops me as I step out of the front door to the parking lot. I see no one. I walk approximately 30 yards to the palmetto strand and duck into them. Another few steps has me standing by the side of the Honda opening the drivers-side door. I hop in and insert the key into the ignition. But it suddenly hits me—I can't leave without attempting to find Adriana.

CHAPTER 36

October 3, 2008 10:30 p.m.

As I sit behind the wheel, I feel this sudden wave of emotion pass over me. The fear is replaced by something else. Something I've never felt before. There's a coppery taste in my mouth and my vision seems to have this reddish tinge. These fuckers know where she is and they're going to tell me.

I step out of the car and go to the trunk. I need something that'll make them talk as fast as possible. I'm reaching for the tire iron when I see a can of hairspray poking out of the top of the disguise bag. I grab them both and head back into Keane Camp room number seven.

Triplett is laying in a pool of blood barely conscious but the other two goons are kicking and moaning through their gags. I walk over and whack both of them on the knees with the tire iron and watch them reel in pain. I grab one of them and ask, "Where's the girl?" A muffled "Fuck-off!" is all I get. I whack his knee again with the tire iron, "Wrong answer!"

I grab the hairspray and the matches from the ashtray and do something I haven't done since high school. The goons' eyes grow wide at the sight of the flame. Certain I have their attention, again I demand, "Where's the girl?"

I don't know where Triplett gets his goons from, but apparently I can't intimidate them. Well, good for them. Still, I feel no reservations for what I'm about to do.

I roll over the fattest of the two goons, unzip his pants, pull them down to his knees and again ask, "Where's the girl?"

He still refuses to talk. I light the hairspray torch again and point the flame at his stomach just below the belt. The smell of burning hair wafts into the air and this time he screams into his gag. His skin reddens and begins to bubble. It's the most disgusting thing I've ever seen. Again, "Where's the fucking girl?"

He sits, moaning in pain but refuses to talk. I lean down into his face and this time tell him, "Next time it's your dick, fuckface!" I step away and light the hairspray and direct the flame toward him. He's bellowing into the gag as I inch closer. The bellowing suddenly stops, replaced by what sounds like "OK, OK."

I set the hairspray down and slowly loosen the ball-gag. He mutters, "The trunk."

"Who has the keys?"

He motions to the dirt bag lying next to him. I move toward him and reach into his pocket, pulling out a set of Hertz rental car keys. The tag says Cadillac on it and the key has 4 buttons—one clearly indicating the trunk.

I tighten the gag back up on my burn victim, tell him if I have to come back his dick is toast, and quickly leave.

Once out the door I hit the panic button on the key and immediately see the car light up. I turn it off and hit the trunk button as I run toward the car. My heart sinks when I see Adriana bound and gagged in the trunk. I carefully pick her up, set her on the ground and begin removing the gag. She's hurt badly.

Remorse and concern mingle with relief and anger. My hands are shaking again as I remove the gag and zip ties binding her. She somehow manages a meager smile and says, "Thanks, Pete."

I look at her, my eyes wet with tears, and tell her I'll be right back. I run back into room number seven, dial the hotel operator and yell into the phone to call an ambulance, that there's a woman in the parking lot who needs help.

Wrecked with emotion, sick with fear, and shaking from adrenaline, I run out the door and notice a couple of people kneeling down near Adriana. Seeing she's being cared for, I sprint to my car and dive into the driver's seat. I start the car, press the gas pedal to the floor and am immediately on U.S. 1 with Keane Camp disappearing in the rear-view mirror.

The drive north to Florida City from Tavernier provides little in the way of services like gas stations, motels, or restaurants. The road is desolate. I slow down to just under 10mph over the speed limit, hoping to avoid attracting attention. Fortunately there's very little traffic to deal with, which gives me time to think. Knowing Triplett is lying in a puddle of blood and his two goons are in serious pain doesn't bother me in the slightest. Oddly, I feel pretty damn good about it.

As I approach Florida City, I make a snap decision to call 911 and report the Keane Camp debacle. Even though it's likely the hotel operator already has, I think it might be a good way for me to get a message to Dave Friedly. He'll eventually figure out it was me there anyway. I pull out one of the unused pre-paid cell phones Gavin gave me. I dial 9-1-1 as I continue heading north on U.S. 1 toward Miami.

The operator answers, and I simply tell her she needs to send an ambulance and the police to Keane Camp in Tavernier. I tell her to have them check room number seven, and they'll find

Jeff Triplett with a gunshot wound and two other men working with him.

I then tell her to contact Dave Friedly with the FBI and tell him this is Pete Johnson.

She begins asking questions. I answer none of them and simply hang up. I roll down the window and toss the phone out. I can hear it shatter into pieces as I head north.

There's not much I'm sure of at this point except the need to get out of Florida. It's a long drive to Interstate 10 and I want to get there fast. Once there, I can go in any direction, which will keep authorities guessing. Hopefully nobody noticed my hurried departure from the parking lot. It was dark, so I don't think they could give a good description even if they did.

As I continue my trek north, thoughts swirl in my head. I'm sickened at the thought of Adriana. I pray she's OK. I'm worried about Gavin and Rob. They've done nothing except help me, and why? I'm hoping Friedly is clean and that handing him Triplett will clear me of the bogus murder charge. I'm scared, wondering if I'll get out of the country before being apprehended. And I'm terrified of being a fugitive with no assistance from anyone.

I begin to pull myself together as I get to the on-ramp for Interstate 95. I continue driving north until the low fuel indicator wakes me from a daze. Mindful of the many cameras installed at gas stations, I choose an old mom and pop place just past several truck stops at the Fort Pierce exit. I check myself in the mirror and am relieved to see my disguise holding up well. With no pay-at-the-pump option available to me, I meander into the scummy little station, grab a soda, some chips and pre-pay for thirty bucks of gas. A kind little Middle-Eastern lady takes my money and tells me to have a nice night. After filling the car, I get back behind the wheel and continue heading north on Interstate 95.

I drive through the night, stopping only for gas and snacks. By the time the sun begins rising, I've motored through Jacksonville and am now on Interstate 10 heading west. When I reach the Alabama border, I realize I need some rest. Fortunately, there are still a few old-time rest stops on this stretch of road. I pull off and park under a shade tree. After a few minutes of stretching, I lay the driver's seat back, climb into the car and quickly drift off to sleep.

Beads of sweat tickle my face as I begin regaining consciousness. I shake my head, reach for a napkin I'd grabbed with the snacks earlier and wipe off my face. The sweat causes my disguise some problems, so I start the car and run the air conditioning for a minute. I lower the mirror and see some wig glue oozing down my forehead. I step out of the car, stretching as I open the trunk and grab the disguise bag. It's hard to fix from the car, but I manage well enough. After buying a soda from a vending machine, I continue my drive west.

As night begins to fall, and with exhaustion overtaking me, I begin looking for the right place to hunker down for the night. Since I can never use the Bernhard L. Motz alias again, I'm not sure if I should attempt a motel check-in or not. I'd given all fake automobile information at Keane Camp so I suspect no problems with the car, but the risk of using a fake name at a motel with no identification to back it up is not worth taking. What's more, if anyone recognizes me and gives my location to authorities, the Feds will have a much better idea where I'm headed.

I'm just across the Texas border when I spot a small KOA campground. Hot temperatures and humid air don't make for a nice night under the stars, but ultimately I decide it's my best option. It's located at an exit along Interstate 10 that time seems to have forgotten. There's a gas station, a couple of fast food restaurants, and an Econo-Lodge. Nothing else.

I check myself in the mirror, again finding everything okay, and make my way into the office. It's nearly 10 p.m., just before closing time, when a middle-aged lady steps over to the counter and asks if I have a reservation. I tell her no but would like to stay the night in a tent camping spot.

She says, "All of our spaces have electricity, a picnic table, a fire pit, and free WiFi—will that be okay?"

"Yes," I tell her. She hands me a check-in card. I use a fake name and then ask to take the card out to the car in order to retrieve the license plate number.

She smiles and says, "Sure, no one seems to remember those numbers." I exit the office, fill out the plate number with two digits wrong, write the make and model as a Toyota Corolla and return with full confidence. She charges me eighteen dollars, hands me a map, and wishes me a good night's sleep.

With no camping equipment at all, I dig through my bags and pull out enough clothes to make a small bed underneath the picnic table. During that process I happen across the last envelope Gavin handed me at the South Breeze. Knowing things can't get much worse, I open it and peer at the contents. I'm not surprised at another wad of cash. A perfect passport with a brand new identity doesn't really surprise me either. But when I open the passport, a small handwritten note is buried on one of the back pages. It simply says "Gavin, I hope this guy finally helps bury Frankel." It's signed, "Cya, G.E.D."

I drift off to sleep on the concrete pad happy about the passport but more puzzled than ever about Gavin, Frankel, and this G.E.D. guy.

CHAPTER 37

October 5, 2008 5:30 a.m.

Stiffness, bug bites, and hunger greet me when I awake. I stretch, grumble, and waste no time in grabbing a few toiletries en-route to the public showers. Knowing my disguise will be ruined in the water, I remove it. Since the sun hasn't quite risen yet, I'm able to shower, put on clean clothes and brush my teeth before anyone is moving around the grounds. Then I turn on my laptop and check the news websites. There's nothing mentioned on any of the national sites. Perplexed, but somewhat relieved that my picture isn't all over the web, I check the email addresses Rob and I have arranged. Nothing has arrived from him either. I'm still in the dark.

I write a brief email to Pete Hoyt, Brett Bower's attorney in Trenton, New Jersey. I attach every file I have, withholding nothing. I tell him that I've never noticed anything in them that stands out other than the few documents Brett found with Nikki's signature. I tell him I have reason to believe Nikki is tied up in this thing somehow, and about the connection between Nikki and Triplett, the retired Miami-Dade cop. I tell him about the incidents in Fort Myers and Tavernier, but I'm careful not to mention Key West. As I'm closing the email, I tell him I sent the original paper files to Dave Friedly of the FBI and that he's welcome to contact him if he'd like. Knowing this is likely the last communication I'll have with Brett, my final line reads: "DON'T SELL BRETT OUT. HE DID NOTHING WRONG!"

With daylight upon me, I load up the clothes I'd slept on last night, dig through the disguise bag for something to alter my appearance, and climb in the car for another day of driving. I pull out of the KOA campground in search of an old, dirty, camera-free gas station. I turn the opposite direction of the interstate and within two miles I find exactly what I'm looking for. Two pumps, an old garage, and a small cash register with no quick store. This place looks like something right out of the sixties. I pull in and pay the attendant thirty bucks for gas. After I fill the car I head into the bathroom with a ball cap, sunglasses, a bleach mix, and a blond colored mustache. Since I'd shaved my head clean two days ago for the wig, I only need to lighten my arm and leg hair, which only takes a minute. Once completed, I attach the mustache, don the ball cap, put on the glasses, and quickly walk to the car. Within minutes I'm barreling down I-10 west toward Houston.

It doesn't take long to hit Houston traffic. It's been a while since I've dealt with rush hour, so it feels like a flashback as my aggravation grows. Then I chuckle a bit considering the circumstances. When I get to the west side of town, I take the Sam Houston Tollway and head south. I'd done a little research this morning in search of a library. I found the Robinson-Westchase public library a few miles south of my intended route. I figure doing some research on Gavin, Rob, and this GED guy might be worth the risk.

I arrive a few minutes after the place opens. The ceilings are tall and there are two large spiral staircases leading to a second floor. The first floor is a huge, sprawling area filled with tables and chairs. The air conditioning feels wonderful, unlike the musty air blowing out of the car vents.

I go to the counter and speak with a librarian, asking where the computers are located. She kindly points me in the right direction. And then I see the microfilm machines. I smile at the technology, but it's part of the reason I decided to stop here. I'm not sure I'll need it, but often an old copy of a newspaper won't be on the internet, but a library will have it on microfilm. With Gavin's history likely coming from the late '70s, it's possible I'll need the microfilm machine.

I sit down at a computer and begin searches on the South Breeze Motel. I pull Monroe County Tax records and get lucky. Its corporate ownership is listed as "Island Rats LLC." I immediately cross reference the LLC with records at The Florida Division of Corporations and find that "Island Rats LLC" is owned by Gavin A. Berge. Then I search G.E.D. A lot of stuff about high school equivalency diplomas, but nothing pertinent surfaces.

I begin searching combinations of names, Rob, Gavin, Frankel, etc., just to see what might pop up. After a couple of hours and every possible combination I can think of, an odd posting appears. I'd searched "Gavin, Bernie Frankel, 1978, G.E.D., and laundromat." An old picture of Bernie Frankel and a guy named George Elliot Dewitt pops up. It's in a newspaper called "The Times of Trenton." Unfortunately the article isn't posted, only the picture, but that allows me to search George Elliot Dewitt. I discover why my new passport is flawless. George Elliot Dewitt is the Director of United States Citizenship and Immigration

Services. He was nominated by George W. Bush in 2007 and confirmed unanimously by the Senate a few months later.

I sit and wonder for a few minutes. What does this mean? It seems obvious that this is the guy who provided my passport. And it's also obvious that Gavin is very well connected. And how on earth did Gavin not notice this note buried in the passport? Or did he mean to leave me a clue?

Baffled, but encouraged, I start trying to figure out the rub between Gavin, Frankel, and Dewitt. There's obviously something very dark between them. I get up from the computer and meander back to the librarian's desk. She looks up through her sexy little glasses and asks how she can help me. I ask if she has any suggestions on how I can acquire an article from 1978 in a newspaper called "The Times of Trenton." She smiles and responds, " Why not try going on-line to the newspaper's website? We can sometimes order that on microfilm but it takes a week or so to get in."

I walk back to the computers and do as she suggested. I quickly strike out as I need a subscription to access old articles and I have no way of making that happen without using a credit card.

It's then I decide to look for more information on Frankel's past. I find a ton of it. While perusing his high school yearbook, I come across an old photo of him and a guy named Andrew that looks eerily similar to Gavin. I dig further in the yearbook and when I find "Andrew's" picture, I'm all but certain it's a very young Gavin. I quickly scribble "Andrew's" full name down on a piece of scrap paper with plans to search that name later.

But now I begin looking for information about Rob. It suddenly dawns on me that I'm not really sure what his last name is. I'd heard several nicknames, and once I heard Gavin address him by the name of Soloman. I start running searches with Key

West, drug smuggling, Bahamas, Rob Soloman, and any other related topic—but nothing noteworthy appears. I start digging around in Key West Senior High School yearbook pictures and look through all of the senior pictures for the years he might have graduated. Luckily, the school only graduates about a hundred students a year, so it only takes me about an hour to find him. His last name does turn out to be Soloman, but the searches I run turn up nothing except that he was a senior at Key West High School. I feel like there's more there but I'm out of ideas how to find out.

By now the day's withering away and I feel the need to get on the road. I also need some time to think. It looks like Gavin has a history with Frankel, but it's not clear what the history might be.

I leave the library, hop on the Sam Houston Freeway north and quickly find myself motoring west on Interstate 10. In short order, I reach Highway 59 and head toward Corpus Christi. I drive to a small town called El Campo and decide to park for the night. There's a little motel called the "White Lodge" just off the highway. It's clean, the security looks weak and it has WiFi. I decide to stay there for the night. I pay with cash and use a false name similar to my new passport to check in. The attendant doesn't notice a thing.

As night falls on El Campo, I drift off to sleep even more curious about Gavin, Frankel, and Dewitt than I was last night. It seems Gavin has a beef with Frankel, and Dewitt seems to be allied with Gavin. But what's the real issue? And how does it even matter to me?

CHAPTER 38

October 6, 2008 7:00 a.m.

I awaken well rested. After the last couple of days it feels wonderful. I step out of the room and walk across the street to a little cafe called Mama Cita's. It has a walk-up window for take-out so I order a breakfast burrito with a cup of coffee and head back to the White Lodge.

With my curiosity about Gavin, Frankel, and Dewitt still running at a fever pitch, I turn on the computer and immediately search for Andrew O'Neal from Trenton, New Jersey. I find a few interesting leads, but nothing stands out. When I add in "laundromat," a short blurb about an O'Neal getting busted for income tax evasion pops up. When I get the name of the Laundromat, I search it and find a story nearly identical to the one Gavin told me one night while we were drinking on Ballast Key. It's now plain as day. Frankel was with the Feds in the late seventies and was involved in the case against Gavin or "Andrew O'Neal," as he was known then.

I sit in silence for a while, thinking about all that's transpired in the last month or so. Gavin and Rob began helping me long before I'd made a connection between elected officials and the financial meltdown. In fact, it wasn't until I was on Ballast Key that I discovered Thrift Bank Mortgage had made campaign donations to Frankel. And while there may be no definitive smoking gun between the two, it opened the door to serious scrutiny of all members of both houses of Congress. Elena put the story on Fox News and it took on a life of its own.

Maybe that's why Gavin is working so hard to help me. Maybe he's just a friend to anyone who could help him get at Frankel. Or maybe he's just a good guy who's happy to help someone, and it's just a coincidence, the connection between me, Thrift Bank, and Frankel. I'm not sure I'll ever know, but I can say with certainty that if I get the chance to burn Frankel, I will.

The sun's blazing through the motel room window around noon when the maid knocks on the door. It's past checkout time, so I grab my things and leave quickly. I hand her a ten-dollar bill for leaving late, and she smiles and says, "Gracias."

I get back on Highway 59 and drive through a few small towns until finally reaching Interstate 37. I'm only on I-37 for a short while when the exit for Highway 77 appears. I feel relief when I see the sign for Brownsville, Texas. My drive is nearing the end.

Pulling into the old border town of Brownsville is almost like being in Mexico. The buildings are old. Nothing looks modern or even maintained. The streets are littered and oily, and the people look downright seedy. The closer I get to the border, the more payday loan stores, pawnshops, and buy-here-pay-here car lots I see. The only redeeming quality about this place is its proximity to South Padres Island. A short 20-minute drive from Brownsville will put you on this beach, one of Texas' most beautiful.

I'm within walking distance of the border crossing when I spot a motel that looks less seedy than the rest. I pull into the parking lot, careful to remain a few spaces away from the lobby door. I dig out the new identity Gavin and George Dewitt arranged for me before I left Key West. I'm nervous to use it because it's the last one I have. I spend a few minutes looking over the picture and memorizing the name and address information. Gavin used a picture of me that he took when I was wearing a very slight disguise. Remembering that disguise, I dig into my bag of tricks and retrieve the wire rim glasses worn in the picture. I walk into the lobby and ask for a single room. The clerk obliges and within a few minutes I have a room key and a place to sleep for two nights. I'll need them both while I plan my exit from the good ole USA.

It's early evening in Brownsville by the time I settle into my room. The motel, Border's Best Value Inn, sits on North Expressway 83, just a mile from the border crossing into Mexico. If it's Border's Best, this place is in real trouble. There are countless restaurants within walking distance, but the area is so sketchy I decide to drive down the street to a Burger King. The drive-thru has no line so I take advantage of the speedy service and immediately head back to the motel.

I sit in front of the TV, eat my Whopper and watch the news. Again, nothing about what happened in Tavernier. I open my laptop hoping to find an email from Rob.

My lucky day! Rob says Adriana was beaten to within an inch of her life. She's in serious but stable condition at Keys Medical Center in Marathon, Florida. He adds she'll likely make a full recovery, but it's going to be a long road. My heart sinks. I knew she looked rough when I pulled her from the trunk, but I didn't realize how serious it was. My stomach knots up so bad I throw my meal in the trash. I sit on the bed tearing up. I can barely finish reading the email.

He finishes by saying something odd is going on with the whole scene at Keane Camp. Nothing has been reported and his contacts in the area have no inside information.

I acknowledge his email by saying thanks, knowing that "thanks" is never enough. I tell him I'll be in touch as soon as I can, but that I'm going off the grid soon. He likely knows this, but I'm at a loss for words. All I can think about is Adriana.

With little energy left, I drift off to sleep with the TV on. The next thing I know the sun is burning through the window and I realize it's 10 a.m. Blocking out everything that's happened the past few days, I hop in the shower and get dressed for what will likely be a busy day.

My new identity is Mike McDermott from Atlanta, Georgia. I pull out the disguise bag and update my appearance to the photo Gavin used on my new passport. I complete the ensemble with wire rim glasses, look in the mirror and hope the next two days go smoothly.

I fire up the computer again and run a Google search for buy-here-pay-here car lots. A slew of them pop up, so I check the locations and find one a mile down the highway. I'm sure it's one I passed on the way into town yesterday.

In the envelope I opened when I was at the KOA campground two nights ago, Gavin left a note about a couple of things I needed to do if I planned to leave the country through Mexico. I guess he knew I'd end up needing to hide. It only made sense that I'd use Mexico as a conduit. He suggested selling the car at a low rent car lot. He titled it under the McDermott alias and left the title in the envelope. He wrote this was the least suspicious way to dispose of it. Driving a perfectly good car to the salvage yard might arouse suspicion, and leaving a car parked somewhere for an extended period of time might eventually result in a call to the authorities to investigate. I write down the address and phone number for the dealer and set it aside. That will be my last stop of the day.

Next, I run another search for a men's store. I need to find a money belt. Gavin knew I'd need money if I were going to hide. He left plenty in the envelope and suggested I hide it on my person, maybe a money belt. There's a leather shop not far from here so I scribble down directions on the sheet of paper with the car lot address.

Finally, I look online for where to get the application for something called an "FMM" tourist card. Gavin wrote that the most important thing to do was to acquire a "Forma Migratoria Multiple" or "FMM"—tourist card. Since I'll be leaving the border tourist zones, officially within 15 miles of the border, and staying in Mexico longer than 72 hours, it's required. A police officer can ask for it at any time, and if I don't have it, it means a fine and likely a trip to the police station.

The application must be turned in when I enter the country. They then issue the card and I'm required to keep it with my passport. This adds a wrinkle to my border crossing because it's another chance for someone to recognize me. Still, Gavin felt it was less risky than traveling in Mexico without it. I'm glad he brought it up. I had no idea. The search provides several suggestions for acquiring the paperwork, and it can even be downloaded and printed at home. Since I don't have a printer, I search for the nearest FedEx office and scribble the directions on my list of places to go.

In his note, Gavin also suggested a couple of South American countries for residency. He and I are thinking along the same lines. The dollar goes a long way in those countries. That was one reason my sister and I took a trip there many years ago. We stayed two weeks and visited two different places. The airfare was the most expensive part of the trip. I plan to go where I've been before. Even though it's been 10 years, at least I know a place I can hide in plain sight.

With three errands mapped out, I get up, don my baseball cap, adjust my wire rim glasses and head out, hoping none of this takes very long.

CHAPTER 39

October 7, 2008 noon

It's around noon when I finally walk out of Border's Best. The smell of car exhaust wafting up from the expressway is enough to make me gag. I walk quickly to the car and keep the windows up and the AC on.

Luckily, all of my stops are within a couple miles of the motel, so the day moves quickly. The FedEx staff is very helpful. The store manager is bilingual and knows the Mexican travel laws well. He actually assists me in filling out the FMM form.

Next stop is the leather store. I never knew there were so many styles and choices in money belts. I employ the "blend in approach" and purchase a no style work belt. As I'm walking out, I notice a luggage store across the street. A picture of a backpack reminds me that I'm going to need one. I walk in and buy the biggest and best. I feel lucky to have seen the place.

Before heading to the car lot I make a quick stop at the motel. I clear out all the crap remaining in the car. Some will be thrown away and some kept. I'm just not sure how to pack for being on the run, and I want some time to sort through my stuff.

This last stop makes me nervous. I suspect there are surveillance cameras all over the place. Then again, I'm likely on cameras at the leather and FedEx stores already. As long as no one is suspicious I should be okay.

The lot I picked this morning is called "Cheap Chariots." The building looks like it was a fast food joint in a past life, but has since been "updated" to accommodate "Cheap Chariots." I walk in and am nearly knocked off of my feet by the smell of stale cigarette smoke. This makes me happy, as it tells I'm in a low rent business. They're likely more interested in my money than anything else.

A heavyset Hispanic woman approaches me and asks how she can assist. I act down on my luck and say I want to sell my Honda. She masks her pleasure well but I can see the wheels turning in her mind.

She asks how much I want for it and I tell her I'd like the blue book wholesale price. She uses the flinch technique of negotiation by acting as though that price is physically painful to her.

Knowing what she's doing, I immediately come down on the price. She then asks to drive the car and I agree. We get in and she drives north on the expressway for a few miles and turns around. On the way back she makes small talk by asking why I need to sell it. I tell her I'm moving to the area and I need the money to get started here in Texas. She asks how I'll get around. I simply tell her my girlfriend has a car and that we plan to get by on hers for now. It's a simple generic story.

I say no more as we head back to the lot. Once there, she has me take a seat in her office as she pulls out the blue book and shows me the price she can pay. I use the flinch technique back on her and she counters it properly by saying she should actually be offering less. I'm laughing in my mind knowing she's bargaining in a textbook way. I agree to the price. It's $1,400 but only if she pays cash. She agrees.

A few minutes later I find myself walking down dirty, nasty North Expressway 83 toward Border's Best. This entire town is disgusting, and I can't wait to get out.

CHAPTER 40

October 7, 2008 5:00p.m.

The walk to the motel takes about 30 minutes. It's a bizarre feeling. I'm homeless, I have no wheels, no job, and I'm wanted for murder and questioning in a mortgage scandal. And if that weren't enough, it's possible there's several new charges pending from the incident at Keane Camp in Tavernier.

Since this evening and tomorrow afternoon are likely the last 24 hours of having reliable cell phone and Internet service, I start making some calls. I'm curious about Elena. There's still no story airing on the news about Tavernier. Surely she knows something. I pull out the satellite phone left over from Ballast Key and dial her. Naturally it goes to voice-mail. I leave a message that I'll call her back around 6 p.m., hang up, and turn off the phone.

I then turn on the last of my disposable phones and dial the South Breeze for a chat with Gavin. He answers quickly.

It's good to hear the old man's voice, but it's also hard not to call him by his real name, Andrew O'Neal. His story and motivation in all this have been on my mind since discovering the link between him, Dewitt and Frankel. But over the last couple of days I've realized it doesn't really matter. I hope to have a conversation with him about Frankel and Dewitt someday, but I have no idea when that will be.

I immediately tell him it's the only time I've used this phone and he responds, "Good." I ask how Adriana is. He tells me she's improving. I ask what's coming out of Tavernier? He says, "Sit down, Pete." A lump builds in my throat as he continues.

"You killed Triplett. He didn't make it until the police and ambulance arrived."

My heart skips a beat. I just assumed he'd somehow survive. Oddly, I don't feel bad about it. I just don't want any more trouble.

Gavin breaks the silence with a piece of good news. "The Feds came in and took over the investigation from the Sheriff's Office. They've kept it all very hush-hush. They put out a press release that an armed intruder was shot and killed in eastern Monroe County at Keane Camp."

He continues, "Pete, they waited to release the information until this morning and it barely made page 3 of the paper."

I ponder what this means for a minute when Gavin chimes in again, "Pete, I think they're figuring out you didn't kill that guy in Miami. Otherwise there would be another news report out on you now, because they know you were there."

He's right. But that doesn't mean they aren't still looking for me in a big way. "I've still got to keep moving, Gavin. I've got no idea what they want from me over all of this. I'm headed south and I'll be in touch. I'm going to need a good lawyer. Do you know anyone?" I ask.

"I'm a step ahead of you, Pete. Just keep communicating by email, and we'll handle things here."

He finishes the conversation abruptly by saying, "Good luck and Godspeed my friend."

The conversation takes less than 2 minutes. Not surprising since short calls are a rule both he and Rob have pounded into my head.

I sit in silence for a few minutes. My range of emotions run the gamut. Sick about Adriana; somewhat happy about Triplett's fate; depressed at the finality of my conversation with Gavin; and finally, relieved knowing he's already working on the legal end of this mess.

It's a little after 6 p.m. when I re-dial Elena on the satellite phone. This time she answers immediately. "What the hell happened down there, Pete? And where are you?" she says.

"No need to worry about where I'm at Elena. Why no story in the news? Why isn't my name plastered all over the airwaves?"

She tells me about the call she made to Dave Friedly. She says that she was able to confirm to Friedly that the picture I sent her was the same man she saw leaving Nikki's house. She also told Friedly that he was the same man who was chasing me in Fort Myers.

"Friedly confirmed to me his name is Triplett. Friedly went to Keane Camp. Apparently the two guys you tied up won't talk, but they have ties to organized crime."

"Pete," she pleads, "According to Friedly, this likely runs deeper. He's not sure how deep it goes, but he knows you didn't kill your boss. He needs to speak with you."

I sit and think for a moment. Contemplating a major move in a few minutes isn't easy or smart. I can't help but think my leverage is better if he doesn't have me in custody. I've already overnighted what's left of the original files. He has Triplett's accomplices, Triplett is dead and I don't know what more I can tell him. Fuck him, I decide. I'll work through this from a distance.

"Elena, this is our last conversation. I'm sorry but I don't believe Friedly knows what's going on yet, and I'm not going to trust my life to this guy. I've honestly given you all of the files I have. By now Friedly has the originals at his office, and the flash-drive I gave you at Last Chance. Until the Feds figure out how to clean this mess up, I'll be somewhere else. Goodbye Elena, and thanks."

"Pete," She says, "Senator Frankel is stepping down today. Speculation is that many more members from both houses will be forced to do the same. A lot who don't step down will likely lose re-election. Thanks for the story, Pete."

I thank her again for her help and before she can say anything else, I hang up.

With all of the communications I needed to make complete, I walk across the street to some joint called "China Wok" and order some Cashew Chicken. I head back to the motel, eat and begin planning my journey.

CHAPTER 41

October 8, 2008 7:00 a.m.

The sun rises early in the stinky little town of Brownsville, Texas.
Doors slamming, kids screaming, and horns honking. Who needs
an alarm clock? The Griswalds must have gotten up early for their
day trip into Mexico.

I hop in the shower and in a few minutes I'm cleaned up and
rummaging through my things in an effort to decide what travels
with me, and what gets thrown in the dumpster.

I spend an inordinate amount of time going through the
disguise kit. From now on the disguise is fairly simple. Very short
hair bleached as white as I can get it. This includes eyebrows,
arms, legs, and facial scruff. The wire rim glasses round out the
disguise. Today I re-attach the scar for good luck.

I pack clothes, toiletries, and any items I have left over from
Thrift Bank. The computer fits nicely in a side pocket of the
pack. Within two hours of waking up I've dressed, packed and
researched the bus schedule I plan to use to get to Mexico City.

The bus leaves in three hours so I need to get going. The
biggest issue is crossing the border and getting my FMM card for
travel. I haven't used the new passport for anything except Border's

Best Motel, so I'm anxious about using it at the border crossing. If anything goes wrong there, I'm likely headed to Friedly's office in Washington, D.C. A place I have no desire to visit.

My last task before leaving is to place all of my cash, except what I need for the bus ticket and some food, in the money belt. The cash Gavin gave me fills the belt, but it works perfectly. No one will have any idea what the belt holds.

I walk out the door and drop off the key at the office. Border's Best has seen the last of Pete Johnson, aka Mike McDermott.

The walk to the border takes approximately 30 minutes. I stop for coffee and a muffin in a local shop. In Brownsville fashion, the coffee's cold and the muffin's stale.

The line entering Mexico at mid-morning is non-existent. I take a deep breath, walk into the border patrol office, and politely ask where I can obtain an FMM card. A large Mexican points toward the other end of the building where several other Americans are waiting in line. This is good, I want to blend in. I join the back of the line and wait. It doesn't take long before a dark haired guy named Alexis looks at me and says, "Let me see your paperwork, senor." I hand him my passport and the form I'd filled out at the FedEx office two days ago. He looks at them and asks for my destination. "Mexico City," I tell him. He stamps the form, hands over my documents and says, "Have a nice visit, senor."

Breathing a sigh of relief, I walk out of the border office, grab a cab, and it's off to "Central de las Autobuses." I tell the driver I want to be dropped at El Expresso Bus Company.

"No problemo, senor," he says.

It takes about twenty minutes, winding through old dilapidated neighborhoods and areas where poverty looks generations old. Finally, we pull up to the station. I pay the driver and make my way to the El Expresso ticket purchase window. I buy a first class ticket on a bus to Mexico City. It leaves in forty five minutes.

First class leaves a lot to be desired in the Mexican bus system, but at least the bus is air-conditioned and has a bathroom. Luckily, I'd held onto my iPod throughout this ordeal, and even remembered to charge it last night. I find a seat close to the front, sit down, stick in the ear buds and fire up some tunes. I'm out of the U.S. now and headed to Mexico City. With any luck, I'll be out of Mexico soon.

CHAPTER 42

October 10, 2008

For the next two days I ride through towns like Jimenez and Padilla, heading south over bumpy pothole-filled roads. And the term road is an overstatement. I switch buses in a town named Gonzalez due to a brake problem, and again in Tampico due to an overheating issue. By the time I see a mileage sign to Mexico City it's been two days.

We're on Highway 105, getting close to a town named Pachula de Soto when the bus abruptly pulls over. I remove the ear buds when two Mexican Federales board the bus. They briefly confer with the driver before walking down the aisle questioning several passengers. My palms are sweating as they pass me on their way to the rear of the bus. On their way out they look down at me and grumble something in Spanish before finally stepping off the bus. I relax when they motion to the driver he's free to go.

Exhaustion from the bus ordeal is wearing hard as we near Mexico City. The bus is headed to the central terminal, which is fourteen kilometers west of the international airport. From there I plan to grab a cab to a nice hotel. I'm not sure yet where that will be, but I figure a good cab driver can solve the problem for me.

Watching the scenery near Mexico City pass by, I think about Adriana. I haven't been able to access email or a phone since leaving Brownsville, and I have no idea how she's doing. She's my only real concern. While I'm still apprehensive about getting caught and landing in a Mexican jail, her recovery worries me most. This Mexican road trip has given me a lot of time to think about everything that's transpired over the last month or so. Knowing I've got just one more stressful journey to make before I land in a safe place gives me some solace. If I can make it, I should at least have a chance to catch my breath, rest, and, if necessary, hide out indefinitely—and that beats jail.

I'm only 10 miles from the terminal when the bus breaks down again on a busy six-lane highway with traffic jammed on both sides. It's torture but there's nothing I can do except wait. It takes two hours before another bus arrives. Finally, we arrive at El Expresso in the central terminal of downtown Mexico City.

I want to deal with as few people as possible, so I grab a cab, and in my broken, sorry excuse for Spanish, ask: "Hotel near Aero Puerto?"

"Si, senor," he replies.

We fight our way through heavy traffic until he pulls into a dumpy little place across from the main road running in and out of the airport.

I look at him and say, "No Gracias, Senor." I spot a nice looking high-rise down the road and point to it saying, "Blanco."

He smiles, "Si, Senor."

In a few moments we're pulling into the Al Hombre Airport Hotel. I pay the driver his fare plus another ten bucks. He enthusiastically raises his hand and says, "Gracias!"

After the sweaty, stinky cab ride, the Al Hombre air conditioning is refreshing. The front desk staff is cordial, and fortunately they have a room available. It's a hundred bucks American, which is expensive for Mexico, but at this point I don't care. It's a nicer place than I would normally stay, and when they ask me for a credit card I simply tell them cash. They don't seem to miss a beat when I pay them for the night and a little extra for the key deposit. I ask where the hotel restaurant is and they point me in the general direction. I head straight for it.

The TV's tuned to CNN in Spanish which perturbs me, but I'm hungry, tired, and don't really give a shit. I order some local cuisine, eat, tip the hot little waitress and catch the elevator to my room. Stretching out on a big bed in an air-conditioned quiet room, feels great.

Chapter 43

October 11, 2008 10:00 a.m.

By the time I wake up and open the floor-to-ceiling drapes, the sun is well over the horizon. Check-out time is only an hour away. I call and ask for a late departure. They kindly agree.

I open my laptop and start checking on flights to San Jose, Costa Rica. As I hoped, there are several leaving this afternoon. Aero-Mexico seems the best fit, as they have one at 4 p.m. that arrives around 6 p.m. It'll still be daylight in San Jose, which gives me time to find a place to stay for the night.

I check email. Rob sent one yesterday and it was brief. He says Adriana's improving—still no word on Keane Camp debacle. The last line read: "Your attorney is in contact with Dave Friedly."

That's great to know, even though I have no idea who my attorney is. I knew Gavin was working on that, but it seems quick for contact to have already been made. I answer Rob's email with a simple thanks and let him know I'm OK and that I'll be in touch again soon.

I turn on the TV in my Mexican mausoleum and hope like hell I can find the Fox News Channel in English. I'm curious if Elena has reported anything new. It takes some channel surfing, but they have it. The news is full of the typical Mid-East problems, grizzly murders, and the ongoing financial meltdown. Elena does another short piece on government involvement in the housing bust, but it seems like the story is going nowhere. It's like she's stuck. Again, nothing is reported on the Thrift Bank debacle. Since I'd given her a lot more information about Thrift Bank, and me in particular, I'm perplexed as to why she isn't using it. At this point, I really don't give a damn. I need to get out of Mexico, and that's all I care about.

It's nearly noon by the time I hop in the shower. I make quick work of it, and in no time I've got the disguise kit out. The process has become routine. Bleach, a scar and a choice of eye-wear. I pack up my things, extract enough money from the belt to eat, pay for the airfare, and another room if I make it through customs in Costa Rica.

A cab to the airport is readily available when I ask the doorman. I tip him a five-spot, he nods his head with approval, and in minutes I'm being dropped off at the Aero-Mexico baggage handlers kiosk in front of the terminal. I pay the driver and, with some trepidation, enter the airport.

It's a busy day. The lines are long, but instead of being aggravated, I'm relieved. More people means less time for anyone in a position of authority to focus on me. After nearly forty-five minutes in line, I'm greeted by a gorgeous Mexican girl asking me where I'm headed today. I tell her San Jose, Costa Rica, and she asks for my ticket. I tell her I'd like to purchase a round trip ticket. She smiles and asks for my passport.

She asks, "How will you be paying for this today, Mr. McDermott?"

I open my wallet and pull out cash. Fortunately the price is only 4,120 Pesos, which is the equivalent of approximately $600 at today's exchange rate. She asks if I'll be checking a bag and I immediately answer yes. She charges me another $50 for the checked bag, which I happily pay.

Since I know it might seem odd that I'm paying in cash, I don't want to add to the oddity by having no checked baggage.

Security at the Mexico City airport is similar to the states. The lines are long with scanners to walk through, and they frisk everyone. The big difference this time. I'm an American flying out of Mexico to another foreign city, which means additional questions. One-way tickets with no checked bags have long been looked at with extra scrutiny, ever since terrorists decided to fly planes into buildings. That's why I elected to buy a round trip ticket earlier. My hope is that security and Mexican customs agents don't see enough peculiarities to give them reason for concern.

When it's finally my turn in the security line I tremble, knowing this could be it for me. If I show up on an INTERPOL list and someone recognizes me through my disguise, I'll be headed off to jail and awaiting deportation.

I draw the short stick this time and end up with the meanest looking, heavyset security agent of the bunch. I'm careful to be ready. I've got my passport, FMM card, and plane ticket with baggage claim check ready for him. He asks to see them, looks up at me after looking at my passport and in perfect English says, "Go to line number three please."

I look to my left and it's clearly marked international travel. With a cold, clammy, nervous feeling, I smile at him and head off to line number three. I place my laptop and small carry-on bag on the conveyor belt. I remove my shoes, belt, wallet, glasses, and the remaining contents of my pockets and place them next to my laptop. I raise my hands to walk through the scanner, and the agent on the other side motions me through. He asks to see my documents again. Since I had them in hand as I walked through the scanner, I simply give them to him. He nods his head and points me to desk number two.

"So far so good," I think. Nothing seems out of the ordinary. I look up to see another Mexican official sitting behind a desk labeled #2. The desk has glass around it, and an opening just large enough to slide documents through for the official to look at. When I approach, he says, " Documents please," with a very thick Mexican accent. I smile and hand him all of my travel documents along with the FMM card.

He looks up a little surprised, which sends a chill down my spine. I have no idea why he's surprised until he smiles and says, "FMM card? You Americans never have that." I maintain a pleasant look, hoping he's pleased when he comments, "I don't get to fine you." Then he smirks, stamps my documents and tells me to have a nice trip.

As he hands them through the opening under the glass, he asks, "Why are you coming back through Mexico City, Mr. McDermott?"

Caught off guard by the question, I quickly reply, "I want to tour the west coast near Acapulco on my way back to the states." He smiles and motions me on my way.

I quickly gather my things and head for the gate. My sense of relief is almost overwhelming.

An hour after getting through security, my flight boards with little fanfare. My seat is next to the window in the rear of the aircraft. As I near it, I put my laptop in the overhead bin, pull out my iPod and scoot up next to the window. When I feel the plane push-back from the gate I crank up some Bon Jovi and begin a private mental celebration, knowing I have only one more trip through customs and I'll be free to disappear into the jungle of Costa Rica for as long as I have to.

The flight lands in San Jose on time. Retrieving my unneeded luggage and clearing customs is a joke. Costa Rican officials simply glance at my passport, look at my customs declaration I'd filled out during the flight, and rubber stamp me into the country for six months.

I grab a cab outside the terminal and ask the driver to take me to a hotel where the ladies are friendly. He smiles and says, "Yes, Amigo." In 15 minutes we're at the Hotel Del Ray. I pay him, grab my bags, and in no time I'm checked into the hotel in my new country under my new name—Mr. Mike McDermott.

CHAPTER 44

Two Years Later

It feels odd sitting in first class on a flight from San Jose, Costa Rica to Washington, D.C., next to Dave Friedly, the FBI agent who's been trying to apprehend me for more than two years. He's a nice guy. Honest and fair. His handshake when we met in the terminal a few minutes ago was firm and warm. He looks just like the picture I found while searching for him on the Internet a couple of years ago. As the airplane taxis to the runway he smiles and asks, "Are you ready to get home and deal with this?"

"I am," I reply, somewhat surprised to find myself smiling back.

He smiles again and turns to look out the window as the engines roar and the aircraft rumbles down the runway.

I sit in silence, reflecting. I'd spent the last two years in a small village called Puerto Viejo. It's on the Caribbean side of Costa Rica, a couple of hours south of Limon, the main port city on the east side of the country. I'd befriended a nice woman named Jenny who owns a small eighteen-room motel on the ocean, aptly named "Jenny's Cabanas." Fortunately, she needed a maintenance man, and since Robnoxious had trained me so well, I took the job. The pay was room and board.

The last two years have become a blur. Motorcycle rides up the coast to the small town of Limon were a twice-weekly event. Limon, with a population of 55,000 people, offered me cover to send and receive emails without the risk of someone tracking the internet IP address to Puerto Viejo. I used at least fifty different locations within the city. It wasn't great security, but in Costa Rica it was the best I could do.

Countless emails were exchanged between Rob and me during those years. Mostly information about how my case was working out, but also word on Adriana and how she was doing. My eyes watered every time the news was good, and my anger would rise when it wasn't. As time went on, I began to realize how much I cared for the girl who once called me a pussy. She made a slow but steady recovery, and is now back to work at Dante's. I'm looking forward to seeing her again, and Rob tells me she's looking forward to seeing me too.

John Wayne Tilton, the attorney Gavin found for me, worked tirelessly to clear up the mess my life became during those early days of the financial meltdown. Shortly after arriving in Costa Rica, I discovered who he actually is. He negotiated the end of hostilities between Key West and the United States Government back in the '80s. He's a piece of Conch Republic folklore himself.

Through Rob, my attorney filled me in on the missing pieces of this whole nightmare.

As it turned out, Dave Friedly *is* a good cop. My paranoia about dirty cops and crooked politicians on the take was only partially correct. Jeff Triplett, the beady blue-eyed bastard I killed at Keane Camp, was indeed a retired Miami-Dade cop. Triplett retired young from the police department only to use his connections within the force to do "security work." When he was discovered dead at Keane Camp, his whole ruse was exposed. Several officers were fired or prosecuted for providing information to him, and for using their positions to help ascertain my whereabouts and that of several other people he was hired to track.

Phone records and bank records *were* used to locate me in Miami. As I suspected, the loud-mouthed northeastern girl did phone in a tip that ultimately made its way to Triplett, which is how Triplett made it to Key West and Friedly didn't. The evidence against Triplett's inside men was overwhelming.

The only comic relief I received while all this information was filtering its way down to me is that the bachelor party boat we tossed the Blackberry in did receive one hell of a welcome in the Bahamas. It turns out both Friedly and Triplett were tracking the phone, but Triplett was tipped that the feds were tracking it too. They nearly ran into each other in Bimini, an island about 40 miles east of Miami. Triplett must have been tired. He'd also killed John that night, and dumped his body in the Intracoastal.

Triplett worked for Don Opitz, the guy from Thrift Bank who left me the voice mail I listened to in Miami. He's a high-ranking lieutenant in an organized crime ring based out of New Jersey. Opitz was the legal owner of Thrift Bank Mortgage. He's a smart guy. He hid his criminal activity by building a nationwide mortgage company that wrote legitimate business, but made its real money in fraudulent, bogus mortgages. He was a rising and ruthless star in organized crime.

Elena also turned out to be a bit prophetic when she said the whole story was bigger than me. She credits me with turning her on to it. It moved her career into the national spotlight. I'm glad somebody got something out of all this.

I was wrong about Thrift Bank being a company owned and supported by a politician. Most of the crooked mortgage companies, and there were a lot of them, were just smart crooks who stole with a briefcase and a pen instead of a gun. The politicians kept their interest silent in order to have plausible deniability in case of an investigation. It worked well for them, as not one has made a perp-walk to date. Eighteen Congressional representatives and six senators ultimately stepped down amid scandals and ethics violations, all related to the massive mortgage fraud and housing bust.

I was surprised to learn how deeply Nikki was involved, and why. She'd grown up with Opitz and went to high school with him. When he bought Thrift Bank Mortgage, it was a much smaller operation. As it grew, he staffed it with friends he could influence, and reliable criminal associates. Nikki was an early hire.

She met John Marris in New Jersey, as he was being recruited away from a competing brokerage to be a district manager for the southeast region, eventually overseeing twenty-one offices in Florida, Georgia, and Alabama. That's probably what attracted Nikki to John, marrying high in the food chain. Nikki thought John was important to Thrift Bank. Turned out, he wasn't.

After their marriage, Opitz enticed Nikki into creating fraudulent mortgages in John's region, rewarding her with large payments off the books. John was never in on it. Whether it was loyalty to an old friend who'd given her a job, or plain old greed, Nikki willingly signed onto Opitz's criminal enterprise.

The pace of underwriting that drove me over the edge strained everyone else as well. Nikki and John's marriage was falling apart, and Nikki worried that John was beginning to suspect what she was up to.

When I made my dramatic departure that morning, it set off a chain of events that ultimately led to two men's deaths, Adrianna being kidnapped and beaten, and two years of my life spent running and looking over my shoulder every day.

It was all because of the files.

It was the mention of the missing files in a government wiretap of Thrift Bank's headquarters that triggered the FBI raids, and Friedly's search for me.

John was royally pissed that I'd taken the files; but it was just business. Nikki, on the other hand, panicked. She called Opitz, worried that I'd somehow figured out what she was doing. Why else would I have grabbed the files, but for evidence? And she shared her concern that John was onto her too.

So Opitz ordered Triplett to find me, recover the files, and deal with John as well. My affair with Nikki was almost tailor-made to pin John's murder on me. Nikki knew what was going to happen when Triplett came to her house and left with John. Why she decided to tell me John left with those guys that night, I'll probably never know. Then again, Nikki wasn't very smart.

I think Nikki may be lucky to be alive. If Triplett had caught up with me, I wonder how long before Opitz would have decided that Nikki represented a liability, and had Triplett arrange for some kind of tragic mishap.

Two years of my life gone, two men dead, and a woman kidnapped and beaten over a box of files that never meant anything. I wish I'd never touched the goddamned things.

Nikki and Don Optiz are going to trial. That's why I'm headed back to the States with Dave Friedly. As part of the deal John Wayne worked out, I'm scheduled to testify against Nikki. Once that's complete I'll be testifying in front of the Senate banking committee about ways the massive mortgage fraud was able to perpetuate itself.

I believe the banking committee hearings are just a way to fool the public into thinking they're doing something to correct the problem. I intend to call bullshit on that little sideshow. They won't like what I have to say. Since not one high-level executive has gone to trial, it's going to be fairly easy to call them out on this farce. I just hope John Wayne dotted his i's and crossed his t's on this deal. Knowing his disdain for the government, I'm pretty confident he's done his job.

For my testimony in Nikki's case and the banking committee hearings, I've been given immunity from prosecution in all mortgage-related issues pertaining to Thrift Bank. The murder of John Marris was ultimately pinned on Triplett, so there was nothing to negotiate. With regard to Triplett's death, it was determined to be justifiable homicide. One of the two men with Triplett that night at Keane Camp received twenty years to life for the abduction and assault of Adriana in Key West. The other agreed to testify against Opitz at his trial and will be entering the witness protection program. Both of those men made full recoveries from the injuries they sustained that night at Keane Camp. Thankfully, nothing was ever mentioned about my coercion technique.

The only real "punishment" I'm facing turns out to be a joke. John Wayne negotiated hard when the Feds wanted to revoke my mortgage license. He made them think they really hurt me by revoking it, and used the revocation to reduce my fine down to $50,000. The truth is, I would never have returned to the mortgage business anyway, and since my stock portfolio nearly tripled since the accounts were frozen over two years ago, 50K just makes me laugh.

Brett Bower's attorney, on the other hand, took the opposite approach. Brett's fine was $250,000 with a one year suspension of his license. He also received five years of probation. He did nothing wrong, but his attorney sucked and he had a family to protect.

Yesterday they removed the freeze on my accounts, which had been in place ever since the Feds started looking for me. My agreement stated that once the freeze was removed, I would return to the United States with Friedly and remain in protective custody until my testimony.

Four Heinekens and three hours after take-off from San Jose, I step off the plane and onto American soil for the first time in more than two years. Friedly and I are greeted by two FBI agents he obviously knows well. We're immediately whisked away in a black Lincoln Town Car.

CHAPTER 45

3 months later

"Pete," Friedly says, "This break in the trial is going to be brief, so I'll be brief too. Some of my superiors have been considering the idea of offering you a consulting contract with the mortgage fraud division. It's not full time work, but it pays like it. You'd be traveling with our team, keeping them focused on areas common to fraud. If you've had any concern for your safety when this is over, this could certainly alleviate that."

I sit in silence pondering the whole situation. I've been holed up in a townhouse near the Georgetown Waterfront District in D.C. since my return to the U.S. Friedly required me to wear an ankle bracelet, but I was somewhat free to roam around, although an agent was always following nearby. I knew they were watching my every move, whether financial, social, or case related. I've been quiet and cooperative, but I'm eager to get rid of these guys. And now they offer me a consulting contract?

During the last two years I've fantasized about this very moment. Wondering over and over again what I'd actually do when I could walk away from this mess. I've spent countless hours researching options. Rob and Gavin worked tirelessly looking for the right opportunity to get me back to Key West. Now I'm thinking about a real job?

"I really appreciate that Dave," I say. "I'm a little surprised, so I need some time to think about it."

He smiles and says, "Sure."

Still dumbfounded, I keep thinking about Friedly's offer. We'd walked out of the courtroom and into a waiting area for witnesses, attorneys and law enforcement. It's quiet but I can hear the muffled sound of business and legal conversations. Friedly sits, saying nothing. I look at him closely. He's wearing an expensive suit, checking his smart phone for messages and sending emails.

It's like a flashback as it hits me. Friedly's a good man, I believe in him. But I don't think I can ever work in an environment where someone has control over me again. I've changed. A job, money, a suit? Not on your life. I've got other plans.

I lean over to Friedly, smile and say, "I just want to finish my testimony. Fuck Nikki and fuck Opitz!" Friedly nods in agreement.

Three more days pass and my testimony is finally complete. Two days later, the jury gets the case. Once deliberations begin, I leave the courthouse with a couple of Friedly's men. Nothing's said in the car, which gives me time to think.

The Senate Banking committee hearings ended up being held before Nikki's trial. They were the fiasco I expected them to be. They were shown on Fox News and C-Span. My picture ended up in the back pages of the USA Today Money section when I told one of the senators I'd searched his name and found he was a minority owner of a small bank in Springfield, Missouri. I asked him if that was a conflict of interest in his policy decisions. He scolded me by saying I was in the hearing to answer questions, not ask them. The place went dead silent. My point was made. That senator did not return. The hearings ended three weeks ago.

Since this whole debacle began nothing's really changed. The real estate business plugs along with foreclosures and short sales being the new buzzwords for those trying to get rich quick. The government instituted a plan called quantitative easing, which simply means printing money. This practice allows the crooks on Wall Street to re-inflate the stock market, which has in turn begun to re-inflate the housing market. Essentially, it's happening all over again. But there's one thing I know for sure—I won't be a part of it this time.

We drive toward the waterfront townhouse and I ask Friedly's guys to make a stop at a grocery store three blocks south of the place. I chuckle just a little, knowing that all of the stops here over the last three months have been my only opportunity to communicate with the boys down in Key West. Since this store sells those little disposable cell phones, I've been able to buy and hide them at will. I get out of the car with one of the agents following close behind. Since my commitments are complete under the agreement made by John Wayne, there's less of a sense of concern by the agents. The only question in their minds is when they'll be done babysitting me. I enter the store and nonchalantly walk toward the meat department in the back. I tell the agent following me I need to use the restroom. He waits at the metal doors near the bathroom.

I enter the restroom, call Rob and tell him to be in front of the townhouse in 30 minutes.

I smile at the agent as I walk out of the restroom still buttoning up my pants. I walk to the front of the store and buy a pack of gum and a coke. We walk out of the store and hop in the car. The agent driving tells me that Friedly is waiting for us at the townhouse.

We pull up and I see Friedly standing in front of the door. As I approach he extends his hand. I oblige and we share a firm, happy handshake. I walk into the townhouse. Friedly follows but motions his men to wait outside. I look at him and smirk, saying, "I guess you're finally done with me, eh?"

"Yes," he replies.

I walk up the stairs and grab my bags. I'd suspected things were going to wrap up today so I packed before leaving this morning. As I'm bringing my bags down the stairs I get a surprised look from Friedly.

He asks, "What's your plan, Pete?"

"For starters, Dave, I'd like this ankle bracelet removed."

He shakes his head, smiling, as I sit down in a chair revealing the thing. He pulls out a key, and quickly removes it.

"You haven't implanted a chip in me have you?" I ask.

"No," he says with a smile.

Again he asks, "What's your plan?"

"I'm leaving," I tell him.

"OK Pete, but know that the offer won't be open forever."

"Thank you," I respond.

"One more thing Pete, that reporter you were working with called me the other day. She left her number and said she'd like to hear from you sometime."

He slips me a piece of paper and then says with a smile, "My goons will take you wherever you need to go."

I pause for a second, raising an eyebrow at Friedly. Rob has been in town for the last couple of days awaiting my release. I've spoken with him a few times, and he's the only person who's ever heard me use the term "Friedly's goons." For just a second I wonder if he somehow had a wiretap on me I didn't know about this whole time. I look at him and reply, "No thanks, I've got my transportation covered. But maybe you already knew that?"

Friedly just smiles.

As I walk out the door, I stuff Elena's number in my back pocket. I smile for a second thinking about the fun I could have with her. But that kind of fun has caused me a lot of problems. Too much has happened in the past couple of years.

I look up and see a clean shaven guy wearing a tuxedo standing next to a black Lincoln Towncar. It's typical Rob and Gavin—always playing the part. I laugh, walk over to the rear door and Rob opens it like a chauffeur with experience. I dive in.

Rob walks around to the driver side, hops in and says, "Where ya wanna go?"

"South! I hear there's a small airstrip on Sugarloaf Key that's for sale, and I know a hot Cuban bartender I'd kill to see!"

Rob points the car toward I-95. The last two years receding like Washington, D.C., into the rear-view mirror.

The End

Acknowledgments

In the beginning I just needed a mental vacation. I sat down and wrote a chapter about a fictitious trip to Key West. Ultimately, that trip became a reality-- minus the fiction. After spending a couple weeks unwinding in Key West, I'd completed the first ten chapters of a novel I had no intention of writing.

My sister-in-law Chantelle Kammerdiener encouraged me to continue. She spent countless hours editing and consulting me on the story line. Without her encouragement and assistance I would never have finished the draft. Thank you, Chantelle.

As time passed, it became necessary to make a trip to Ft. Myers Beach. A special thanks to all of the unnamed locals who sent me to so many places that fit into the story. The staff at Hurricane Hideout was exceptional. Their knowledge of Pine Island history made my research easy and enjoyable!

A special thanks to all of the great Key West locals I was able to meet in the fall of 2009. The staff at Island City Aviation, South Beach Cafe, The Palms Hotel and countless waitresses and bartenders who were always right there with a beer and an oyster!

A special thanks to Rebecca Williamson for her insight, care, and diligence in producing a book cover that blew me away. Dead on insight by a rock-star designer!

Thank you Mary Cook for your editing insights and encouragement.

And then there's Action Dave Rogers. As the completion was getting closer, a major final edit was needed. Thanks to Dave for reading the draft and diving into the project. Without his editing expertise this project had no chance of coming together. Dave's meticulous editing of every word and how it was used helped me hone Pete's personality and shape a finale worthy of reading. Thanks Dave!

ABOUT THE AUTHOR

Shane Kammerdiener is a long-time real estate professional. After a brief foray into the corporate world, he lost his job and livelihood during the financial crises of 2008.

Learning from that experience, he recovered by building a portfolio of rental property in Ponte Vedra Beach, Florida allowing him to leave the corporate world he despised forever.

An accomplished pilot, entrepreneur, and real estate investor, Shane now spends his days riding his bicycle on the sand, writing books, and enjoying the tailwinds that the real estate debacle ushered in.

88291350R00148

Made in the USA
Columbia, SC
02 February 2018